The Lobster War

The Lobster War

Ethan Howland

Front Street / Cricket Books

Chicago

YA
How

Copyright © 2001 by Ethan Howland

All rights reserved

Printed in the United States of America

Designed by Anthony Jacobson

First edition, 2001

Library of Congress Cataloging-in-Publication Data

Howland, Ethan.

  The lobster war / Ethan Howland.—1st ed.

    p. cm.

  Summary: Although he fears being in the water, sixteen-year-old Dain is determined to
be a professional lobsterman, despite pressure from his older brother and widowed
mother that he attend college instead, and despite the fact that someone is sabotaging his
lobster traps.

  ISBN 0-8126-2800-4

  [1. Brothers—Fiction. 2. Lobster fishers—Fiction. 3. Single-parent families—Fiction. 4.
Conduct of life—Fiction. 5. Maine—Fiction.] I. Title.

  PZ7.H864 Lo 2001

  [Fic]—dc21

                                                              00-047619

for Daphne

The Lobster War

My mother taught Eddie and me how to pray when we were little. You needed only three things, she said: a Bible, faith, and a problem, which, she would remind us with a shake of her finger, wasn't even necessary to the business of prayer. Well, I didn't have a Bible and my faith was lacking, but I definitely had a problem.

It was late afternoon, and I was two miles offshore in my lobster boat, the *Rita Marie*, drifting. A rope was knotted around my propeller, and out toward sea, the islands that dot our bay like bird shot were disappearing one by one into a thick blanket of fog.

I murmured a prayer, hoping for one of those miracles I had heard about from my mother. But maybe because I never could believe with all my heart, when I leaned over the stern, the rope was still choking the propeller, just like it was the last time I checked.

I sat down, sighed, and stared at the purple smudge of shore and hills on the horizon. A flock of eider ducks flew over my bow, their wings whirring as they headed for a cove to spend the night.

The weathermen had really gotten it wrong that day. The forecast had called for sun with afternoon clouds and a breeze out of the west. Another clear, sparkling day like we'd been having all summer. Not a word about fog, which was now coming in slow and steady, without a sound.

A wall of thick mist swept over Mackworth's Rock, catching in the tips of the fir trees and turning solid, familiar objects into ghosts. If you reached out to touch them, there'd be nothing there. Soon all I could see was the phantom outline of the island. I nervously rubbed my hands up and down the sides of my legs.

I'd been doing nothing but study the horizon for the last half-hour, watching that fog creep in, knowing I'd be smothered in no time, not able to see where the islands were or the lights on shore. There had to be someone out there on the water heading home who would stop and give me a hand. Someone who would get in the murky water and cut the rope instead of me. I looked at a piece of brown seaweed on my boot and began to pray again.

I know it sounds strange, wanting to be a lobsterman and all, but the truth is I was scared of the water.

My thoughts scattered like minnows when I heard the rumble of an engine from the far side of Mackworth. I jumped to the other side of the boat and leaned forward. The engine got louder, coming right toward me, and I started to relax. I knew almost everyone on the water, so I was sure whoever it was would give me a hand. A boat came around the point, shedding white strands of fog, and as soon as I could make it out, goose bumps rose on my arms and I remembered one of Ma's favorite sayings: Be careful what you pray for.

It was Roger Gribbin, about the only person in the world I didn't want to see. He was crazy and mean like a wild dog. You never knew what he was going to do. He acted like nothing in the world really mattered.

One night last summer, to settle an old score that most people had forgotten, Roger, Bobby Nuckles, and Richard Grimes beat up the sheriff. It was hot, and the sheriff was dozing in his cruiser in the dirt lot next to the Grange Hall. Roger, Bobby, and Richard crept up beside the cruiser, swung open the door, and tossed a blanket over the sheriff's head before he had any idea what was happening. They dragged him out and let him have it. The sheriff was in bed for a week. He never found out who did it and ended up leaving town five months later. Some people said my brother, Eddie, was at the Grange that night, but I didn't believe it. Not Eddie.

Roger pulled alongside my boat. His motor gurgled and snarled. He put his foot on the side of his boat, the *Raptor*, and looked me up and down. He wore yellow rubber gloves and rubber pants and boots. Even in his baggy lobstering gear you could tell he was big, lots bigger than me. His skin was dark from the sun. He had spiky blond hair and blue, unblinking eyes. It was those eyes that scared me the most—not his tattoos or his muscles or the way he leaned too close to you when he talked. It was his eyes.

They absorbed everything, even the light, and they gave nothing back. In some parts of the world people believe that cameras can take a person's soul. Well, when Roger Gribbin stared at you hard, you had to wonder if your own soul was entirely safe. And now the way Eddie hung around with Roger, I wondered whether he had come under Roger's spell.

"Hello, Dain," he said, eyeing the rope trailing behind my boat. "Looks like you got yourself a problem here."

"The rope's jammed in the propeller," I said.

"Must've crossed somebody's line."

"Or the rope was just floating free."

Roger surveyed the water around us. He took a breath. "See that fog?" he asked, his elbow on his knee. "It's rolling in pretty fast."

I nodded in agreement.

"Weather report didn't say anything about any fog."

"Not that I heard."

"Wouldn't want to be stuck out here with a fog like that coming in," Roger said, tapping the screen on his depth finder. "Not without proper gear."

Roger had all the best electronics: GPS, loran, radar, a VHF radio, and a depth finder. His boat was one of the fastest around, and he fished the deep water out at the edge of the bay. It was too far out for me. His boat shined, even in the fading light, and your heart beat a little faster just looking at it.

The *Rita Marie* was more like a jalopy, and I was saving my money for parts to fix her up over the winter. She was smaller and older than most. I was always caulking the sides and tinkering with the motor just to keep her running. I didn't mind that she wasn't the best boat around. She had been Dad's and was named after my mother—it made me feel good to be using her.

We floated idly in the middle of the bay, just watching the fog creep closer. "You got a knife on you?" Roger finally asked.

"Sure," I said, showing him my jackknife.

"That's not a knife," he said. He reached into his cabin and whipped out an eight-inch knife with a black handle and a jagged edge. "Now, this, this is a knife."

He held it by the blade, gave it a flip in the air, and caught it by the handle. He held it out to me. "Use this," he said.

I hesitated.

"What's the problem?"

I shrugged.

"Oh, I forgot," he said. "You don't swim."

"I swim okay," I said.

"Yeah, but you don't like to. Afraid of the water. Eddie told me about that. Said his little brother didn't like to swim because of the seaweed. Hey, I understand. I don't like that slimy stuff, either."

Eddie told Roger that? He talked about me like that?

"Don't worry, I'll give you a hand," he said. He tied our boats together and leapt aboard as quick as a bluefish after bait. I took a step back.

"Come on," he said, holding out the knife. "I'll hold your feet and you cut the rope."

I hesitated for a moment, glancing at the fog, at the knife, and at a faint smile on Roger's face. The thought of swimming in water a hundred feet deep with nothing underneath me but darkness and kelp and who knew what else made my stomach churn. But I didn't have a choice, so I unbuttoned my shirt and took Roger's knife. I leaned over the stern, and Roger grabbed my feet.

"I'll kick my feet together when I need to come up," I said.

"Just cut the rope," Roger said.

Before I could think about what I was doing or take a deep breath, Roger let my legs go forward and I plunged into the sea. The cold water slapped my face. Water rushed into my ears. I opened my eyes a crack, trying not to look down into the dark emptiness below. In the murk, with specks of plankton drifting past my face, I could just see the snarl of rope around the propeller. I stretched as far as I could and slashed at the knot with the knife. Hot needles pricked my lungs—I needed air already. I kicked my feet together for Roger to pull me up. Nothing happened. I kicked harder. I tried to twist around to get my head free from underneath the boat, and then he finally started to pull me up like he had all the time in the world.

"Get it?" he asked.

I gulped air and managed to shake my head no.

"I figured you wouldn't," he said. "Did you open your eyes, Dain? Or were you too scared to do that?"

"I'll get it this time," I said.

"You'd better."

Roger dropped me in again, the salt stinging my eyes. I hacked and jabbed at the rope for all I was worth, but it wasn't doing any good. I was just flailing around. Finally, I stopped myself and ignored my lungs, the dark water, and Roger standing above me. I held myself steady with one hand on the bottom of the boat and took three quick, steady slices. The rope fell free.

When I kicked my legs together, Roger pulled me back on board like he was landing a cod.

"Now, that wasn't so bad, was it?" he said.

"No, not so bad," I said, clamping my jaw tight to keep my teeth from chattering. His knife clattered on the deck when I dropped it.

Roger grabbed the knife, hopped back into his boat, and revved his motor while I tried to dry off with an oil-stained towel. My hands were shaking so bad I couldn't button my shirt.

"You still got them traps up in the Narrows?" Roger asked as I fumbled with my shirt.

I had to think for a second to figure out what he was talking about.

"Yeah. I've got some up there."

"You know, you've got to watch the current along there," Roger said, wiping his knife on his sleeve. "It runs pretty strong. Could take some of those traps, I'll bet."

"I guess it could," I said. The current did run through the Narrows pretty hard when the tides changed, but I had never lost a lobster trap there and hadn't heard of anyone else losing one, either.

"Just thought I'd mention it," he said, untying our boats. "I wouldn't want a kid like you to lose any traps."

Roger revved his engine again and pulled away, leaving my boat rocking in his wake. I watched him disappear into the fog, heading toward home. Then I kicked the side of my boat. Why had Eddie gone and told Roger that I was scared of the water? Why'd he do that?

Chapter 2

I live with Eddie and Ma in a small house on the crest of a hill overlooking the bay. When I got home, Eddie's truck was in the driveway. I ran up the front steps. Eddie hadn't been home in almost a week, and I wanted to tell him all about what had happened, about the fog and getting in the water to cut the rope free, and about Roger Gribbin.

But when I stepped inside, I knew right away that something was wrong. The house was too quiet. Eddie and Ma were at the kitchen table with cups of coffee in front of them. The words they had been speaking, all about me I was sure, were practically hanging in the air like clothes frozen to the laundry line in winter.

"Go wash up," my mother said. "You look a mess."

That was Ma. She told you flat out what she thought. I think she felt that she had to be extra firm, raising Eddie and me and working full time. She had flinty eyes that could stop you in your tracks with just a glance.

I hung my Windbreaker on the coatrack by the door and washed my hands and arms at the kitchen sink. I scrubbed with dishwashing liquid, trying to get the sharp reek of bait off my skin. But no matter how hard I rubbed or how hot the water, my hands smelled all summer of rotten fish.

I dried my hands and sat down at the table. Ma stared at me. Eddie studied the steam rising from his coffee. Honey, our old retriever, got up from her spot by the wood stove and nudged my arm.

"Where have you been?" my mother asked.

"Fishing," I said.

She looked at the clock. "Until eight o'clock?"

"My propeller got tangled in some rope."

"I was starting to worry."

Ma knew how to worry. She was an expert. She used to worry about Eddie all the time. But when he dropped out of school two years ago, she just gave up on him and started worrying about me: my grades, going to church, lobstering. All those things.

"Sorry," I said.

Eddie was wearing his leather jacket like he might leave at any moment. He picked up the cup of coffee he had been sliding back and forth, leaned back, and drained it in one go.

"You're busy lobstering these days, aren't you?" Ma said.

"Yeah, I guess I am," I said. "It's been going pretty good."

"Too busy to finish this?" Ma held out the college application I had thrown away. I was going to be a senior next fall, and Ma said I should be applying for college now. College, grades, tests—for the last year they seemed like the only things Ma talked to me about. Somehow college was going to improve me. In Ma's eyes, I guess I needed improving.

Sometimes I'd come home to find college brochures piled neatly on my bed. They were full of pictures of good-looking students, brick buildings, and green lawns. You wouldn't find someone like me in those pictures with my torn flannels and frayed blue jeans, with fish scales caught in my hair and muck on my hands.

Ma's fingers turned white as she pressed the application on the table, trying to flatten out the wrinkles. "You know where I found this?" she said to Eddie. "In the garbage!"

Eddie raised an eyebrow but didn't look up.

"You're going to fill this out," Ma said. "Tonight."

I glanced at Eddie for help, but his face was blank.

I was sixteen, about to turn seventeen, and the one thing I was sure about, the one thing that made sense, was that I was going to be a lobsterman. It ran in the family. And I was good at it.

I did all right in school. My grades were decent, but I didn't like it there. I was the youngest in our class, and it wasn't really until last summer that I started to grow and catch up with the other boys. I didn't have many friends, and I didn't play sports. Not like Eddie. He always had friends, and before he dropped out of school, he played hockey. He made varsity his freshman year. Boy, could he skate. He used to fly around the rink, checking bodies against the boards, taking shots and scoring goals. No one could catch him.

"I don't know that I want to go to college," I said weakly.

"You have God-given gifts," Ma said, meaning my grades, not my lobstering. "Don't turn away from them."

"But, Ma, all I want to do is lobster," I said. "What's wrong with that?"

Ma's jaw tightened. "Dain," she said, "I didn't raise my sons to be no lobstermen. This family has had enough of that."

I didn't talk back to Ma. I followed her gaze to the picture of my dad that hung in the living room. He died during a storm when I was nine. It was mostly the little things that I remembered about him—his big hands, the whiskers on his face, a rumbling laugh. But Ma, she remembered every-thing, every day, and the picture was a constant reminder. That's why I couldn't talk back.

The clock in the living room chimed, breaking the spell. Ma sighed. Honey nudged my arm again, and I stood up to get her some water.

"That's it?" Eddie said. He was sitting up straight now, looking at Ma. His eyes were splintered, gray and green, like they were breaking into a thousand pieces. "The world didn't end when Dad died. We're all still here, and if Dain wants to lobster, let him lobster. Who knows what the best thing is for him, for any of us? Maybe college is no good for Dain. Maybe it is, but just let him be. Let us be."

"Edward, don't *ever* talk about your father like that," Ma said, the iciest, darkest ocean current running through her voice. "Not ever."

Even Eddie couldn't meet her gaze. He stared silently at his coffee mug.

"This discussion is between Dain and me," Ma said, thinking Eddie was done. "It's nothing to do with you."

"Ain't much of a discussion, is it?" he said, getting up. "But that's the way it always is around here. Everything's always got to be your way."

"That's right, Edward. In my house, everything *does* have to be my way." She glared at Eddie, daring him to challenge her.

"Fine," he said, looking straight into Ma's eyes, taking her dare. "I don't need this house, and I don't need you."

Before anyone could say, "Wait, don't go," or "Let's talk it over," Eddie was out the door. I went to the kitchen window. The last I saw was his silhouette in the cab of his truck as he slid behind the steering wheel. Then the truck door closed, and the light went out.

I turned to look at my mother. She never knew how to talk to Eddie. She was patting her hair into place like he'd gone to Hoppin's General Store to get a gallon of milk and would be back in a few minutes. But we both knew he was really going to visit Roger Gribbin and maybe stay awhile, like he'd done before.

Ma stood, smoothing the wrinkles in her nurse's uniform. "Dain, I have to go to work now," she said. "Fill out that application."

"Yes, Ma." I couldn't say no to her.

"Dain," she said. "I just want what's best for you. You know that, don't you?"

"I know, Ma."

She left for work, and I was all alone. I sat on the floor with Honey, scratching her ear for comfort.

Chapter 3

When I woke up at four-thirty the next morning, it was dark outside and the house was quiet. Ma was still at the hospital, and Eddie's room was empty, the sheets on his bed tucked in tight, just like Ma taught us.

I threw on some clothes for fishing and went to the kitchen. I made coffee and a couple baloney sandwiches. The coffee was for my thermos, which used to be Dad's. I had found it in the shed in a pile of tools under a tarp. It was silver and dented, and paint was chipped off the rim. It doesn't sound like much, but I was sure that battered thermos brought me luck. I always took it with me when I went lobstering—drinking coffee made me feel more grown up, more like Eddie, who couldn't drink enough of it.

Honey stirred from her bed and started nosing around her dish. I fed her, and she wagged her tail. For me, this was the morning routine, moving around the empty house before the sun was up.

In the old days, Eddie made the coffee and the sand-wiches, and we talked about how many lobsters we'd catch, the kind of luck we were having, and which string we'd fish first. Now I had the radio for company. That morning the weatherman explained what I had seen with my own eyes the day before: a front was stalled off the coast as warm, humid air from the south met a blast of colder air from Canada. Because of this, a fog bank hovered along the Maine coastline, closing airports, slowing traffic, and keeping people from the beaches.

The fog didn't matter too much to me—I knew the bay like the back of my hand. I threw on my slicker and went outside, Honey at my heels. She ran smack into me when I halted at the bottom of the front steps. Eddie's pickup was next to the woodshed at a slant, like he had come in a hurry, not caring how he parked.

Honey trotted over to the truck and sniffed around the tires. I followed her and stood by the driver's door, my hood still up against the mist that was settling on the lawn, on the leaves, and on the truck itself. Eddie was slumped behind the wheel. There were a couple beer bottles on the floor and a tube of lipstick on the seat. I tapped on the window, and he opened one eye and rolled the window down.

"What are you doing out here?" I asked.

Eddie looked around like it was the most natural thing in the world to sleep in a truck in front of your house when you have a bed and a room all your own. He shrugged.

I noticed a cut and a bruise above his eye. "What happened to you?"

He touched his forehead and winced. "Oh, it's nothing. Got into a scuffle in town."

Even though I didn't always understand Eddie, I wished I was more like him. The way he moved, even simple gestures like brushing back his long black hair, tilting his head to laugh, or turning his wrist to see the time, was filled with an easy confidence that came from some part of him no one else could see.

"Sorry about running out last night," he said. "I can't take it when Ma tries to make us do what she wants, without even asking what we think."

"I know."

"You fill out that application?"

"Not yet."

"You just do what you want to do."

I nodded. "Why don't you come in and get something to eat?"

"No. I don't want to be around when Ma gets back. I just wanted to pick up some stuff."

"Yeah?"

"Roger said I could move in with him. I figured it would be better for everyone."

I shuffled my boots in the dirt and didn't say anything. I had wanted to tell Eddie about Roger and the propeller. I had wanted to ask him why he told Roger about my fear of the water. But those thoughts evaporated with Eddie's news. He was leaving.

"Where you off to?" Eddie asked.

"Hauling," I said.

"In this weather?"

Mist swirled around us. "Sure," I said. "This is nothing."

"School's starting soon," Eddie said. "Guess you'll be pulling the traps up for winter, huh?"

"Not yet," I said. "I'm keeping them in a while longer. I've been doing pretty good this summer. No sense in stopping now."

"I guess not."

"So, when are we going to see you?" I asked.

"I'll be around," he said. "Don't worry about that."

"I gotta go," I said. "I want to get out there before the wind kicks up. Why don't you go in? Your bed's made."

"Sure," Eddie said, rolling up the window. "See you later."

I took the path through the woods. It was still dark and foggy, but I didn't really notice. I was lost in a fog of my own. Eddie was moving out. I knew he'd been leaving us for a while, but now he was really doing it.

Eddie and me, we used to do everything together. We talked about everything, too: boats, girls, Ma and Dad. I'd ask him questions, one after another. And he'd give me answers. I always felt good when I was with Eddie.

Ma did the best she could, but she worked a lot, and when she wasn't working she was at her church meetings praising the Lord and reading the Bible. There were plenty of things I couldn't ask her. But Eddie was always there.

Dad had Eddie out on the water as soon as he could walk. He taught him to fish, to lobster, to dig clams and worms. After Dad died, Eddie taught me. He showed me how to make a lobster trap, how to steam the slats of spruce and bend them around a frame; how to tie in the netting and pour the concrete slabs that weighed the trap to the seafloor. The shed where we made our traps became like a second home to us. We'd throw some logs in the potbellied stove and work into the night.

Eddie taught me how to lobster, too. At first we fished from a ten-foot skiff, hauling the traps by hand. It was hard, and it was slow, but it was how we learned. Then one summer, Uncle Ray took us to a shed behind his house. Rusty hinges creaked when he swung open the door. The *Rita Marie* was inside.

"She needs some work," Ray told us, pulling a tarp off the bow. "But I think you'll find that she can handle about anything you throw at her."

Eddie slapped me on the back and whooped. "Now we can really go hauling," he said.

"We'll have to build more traps," I said.

"Sure. And get more gear and paint more buoys."

Ray patted the boat gently. "She's a good boat," he said. "Someone should be using her."

But about two years after that, when I was thirteen and Eddie was sixteen, he started to hang out with guys from his own grade more. And then he started lobstering with Roger. He got into more and more fights at school. I'd see him in the halls, and he'd barely notice me. Eddie had lots of girlfriends, never the same one for too long. He didn't talk about them much.

I began to spend more and more time on my own. In the summer, I was on the water. In the winter, I was down at the shed working on the boat: sanding, caulking, and painting. I built my traps, painted my buoys, and got ready for the next season. Now I hardly knew what Eddie did anymore. I tried not to let it bug me.

I came out of the woods and stood at our lot by the shore. Next to the boat shed was a stack of busted pots waiting to be repaired and a rusting shell of a car up on cement blocks, nettles growing through the floorboards. Eddie had towed it there summers ago, swearing he could get it running again. But he had lost interest in it, kind of like how he had lost interest in me. I guess better things had come along.

Past the shed, the wharf pointed into the fog, which blanketed the water so thickly I could hardly see. It made familiar noises stronger and stranger. Waves tumbled onto the stone beach, and rope creaked against wood. Then a patch cleared in the fog, and I could see the *Rita Marie* on her mooring beyond the wharf where she could still float at the lowest of tides. She rode low in the water, her nose rising sharply at the front. Her boxy cabin held a pocket of warm air and kept out the salt spray. She was all I needed. Then the fog shifted, and she became a vague outline again, not entirely there.

A gong buoy clanged through the mist. I steered southeast toward Gannett Island, where I had some traps. A gull settled on the cabin roof, waiting to scavenge for food when I picked through my traps and threw the old bait over the side.

I poured myself some coffee from the thermos and relaxed. The water was calm. An orange sun rose above Pinkham's Head, glowing weakly through the fog. The in-board motor thrummed through the soles of my boots. It made me feel better to be on the water. Everything was clearer there. That's all I wanted, for things to be clear and simple, like they used to be when Eddie and I were always together.

By the time I got to Gannett, the fog had thinned, and I spotted one of my green-and-orange buoys beneath the fifty-foot cliffs along the island's edge. I brought the boat alongside the buoy, keeping an eye on the cliffs about twenty feet away where waves sloshed in the crevices between slabs of barnacle-covered rock. I threw the engine into neutral, hooked the buoy with my gaff, and swung the rope onto the hydraulic spool, which started to pull up the traps from the seafloor. I watched beads of water run down the waterlogged rope and wondered if I'd have a good day.

Lobstering isn't too complicated. It takes work—hard work—and a little luck doesn't hurt. The traps I used were really just wooden crates, flat on the bottom and rounded on top, with a hole for the lobster to go in. Most lobstermen used wire traps, but I was sticking with the wood ones, like my dad had used. Anyway, the principle is the same. You put some fish in a bait bag inside the trap, sink it onto the seabed, and hope some lobsters will crawl into your trap to get at the bait. If they crawl in, they are led down a funnel made of netting. Once they're inside, they're pretty much stuck, and you've made some money. If they don't go for the bait, well, you set the trap again and hope for better luck.

Around here, we mostly lay the traps in strings—that means six or seven traps tied together by rope—and at the end of the string, there's a rope attached to a buoy for you to grab to pull up your traps. The buoy is the only thing connecting you to your traps. If that buoy gets lost in a storm or to the tide, you try to find your traps by dragging a grappling hook on the bottom. But if your hook doesn't snag any rope, those traps are gone. Who knows how many lost traps are sitting on the bed of our bay? A fair few, I'd bet.

I had almost two hundred traps myself. There were guys with five and six hundred, and some lobstermen had the full state limit, eight hundred. They were the ones who fished year round. That would be me one day. For most guys, the season for lobstering ran from spring until late fall when the water got cold and the lobsters moved to deeper territory. I usually pulled my traps up before school started, but this year I was doing so well that I was planning on going longer.

Suddenly, the first trap came out of the green sea, dripping water between the slats. I swung it onto a rack that ran the length of the boat and opened the trap door. Inside the trap there were a handful of crabs, some spiral-shelled whelks, and a sea urchin, which were all useless, and what looked like a keeper—a lobster over the legal size limit, three and three-sixteenths inches long on its back. If a lobster is too small, you have to throw it back. If it's over five inches long, you throw it back. If it's a female carrying eggs, back it goes. And if it's got a notch in its tail—a cut a lobsterman makes marking it as a breeding female to keep the stocks up—she goes back in. There are lots of lobsters that you can't keep, at least not legally.

I whipped out my brass gauge to measure the lobster. It was a keeper, all right. I held it up, watching the light shine off its shell, green, brown, and blue. It flapped its tail and pawed at the air with its claws. If a lobster muckles onto your hand with one of those claws, you really know it. I put rubber bands around the lobster's claws to keep it from fighting and dropped it in a basin of water. I chucked the crabs and whelks and the urchin into the sea and took a fresh bait bag, stuffed with salted red fish and herring, and put it in the trap, which I slid to the end of the rack, ready to go.

As I swung the rope onto the spool to bring up the next trap, I checked the depth finder. I was in fifteen feet of water. I'd have to see what else I caught in the string to decide if I should move it to a deeper spot. The thing you have to decide with your traps, whether you have eight or eight hundred, is where to put them. Lobsters move around a lot, traveling from one part of the bay to another, so you have to keep moving your traps, trying to figure out where they're likely to be next.

You also have to be careful not to lay your string of traps over someone else's, or move in on their territory. Lobstermen hate it when someone messes with their traps. If you touch someone else's traps—and people do sometimes, either to steal lobsters or see how someone is doing in a certain part of the bay—they'll go after yours, and just like that you can have a lobster war on your hands, with buoys getting cut and traps being dragged out to sea.

Even breaking into lobstering can be hard. You hear

about men who buy a boat and all the gear and begin setting their traps. And then they start losing their traps, or maybe a skiff disappears, or sometimes boats sink during the night. No one talks about it much. Everyone keeps their suspicions to themselves. That's the way it is around here.

Eddie and I were all right when we started because of Dad. Everyone knew him. He had been fishing for years, so no one gave us any trouble. Even so, I didn't want to get involved in any kind of lobster war, even by accident, so I tried to steer clear of where everyone else was. In the summer, parts of the bay bristled with buoys, there were so many traps. Mostly, I looked for out-of-the-way areas, with ledges for the lobsters to hide in during a storm, but also a flat bottom for them to feed on. This season I had found some pretty good areas where no one else was fishing. I was doing all right.

The second trap in the string surfaced, and I heaved it onto the side of the boat. This one had a short lobster, which I threw back, and a sculpin, a fish with red skin, bulging eyes, and a gaping mouth as wide as its head. I lifted it out of the trap carefully, not wanting to get stuck by one of its spiny fins, and flung it into the water. I shivered as it swished its stubby tail, darting to its home among the kelp on the seabed.

I rebaited the trap and moved it down the rack next to the first one. Already the deck of the boat was getting messed up with the seaweed, mud, and algae that dripped from the traps. Before I started to bring up the next trap on the string, I saw that I had drifted closer to Gannett, and I eased the boat away from the churning water at the base of the cliffs. Once I had put a little distance between my boat and the island, I went back to the traps and hauled in the third crate.

It made me feel good to be out lobstering on the bay. I knew the craggy islands and the currents. I knew the *whoosh* of air through the feathers of a gull and the smell of waterlogged rope drying in the sun. The bay felt like home, and I could understand it, even though I was scared of the water itself.

I think it was the darkness. Around here, the water is murky. You can hardly see into it; not like in those pictures of coral reefs where you can see for miles and colorful fish swim through bands of light. The ocean here is dark and deep and full of things you cannot see.

It made me uneasy to think about the water too much. I'd picture my boat sitting on the surface: a hull twenty feet long, just wood and caulk between me and the water. And then I'd think about the boats that were right at that very moment sitting, leaning, decaying on the ocean floor. There were sunken ships—schooners, tankers, and lobster boats—in and around the bay, up and down the coast. And then I'd wonder, what's keeping my boat on the surface? What's the difference between the *Rita Marie* and the boats on the bottom of the ocean? A sudden wave? An unseen rock? A rising swell? When I thought about the ocean too much, it made me feel alone. All that water, running so deep. All that darkness, going on and on, forever.

I finished pulling up the string, got two more lobsters, and brought my boat around to reset the traps in slightly deeper water. I gave her some gas, dropped the lead trap over the side, and stood clear as the other five traps and the buoy flew off the stern to their new spots on the bottom of the bay. I'd be back the next day to see how I'd done. Maybe the traps would be full. Maybe they'd be empty. Each day was a little different from the last. That was one of the things I liked about lobstering.

By noon I was cruising toward the Narrows, followed by a small flock of gulls, and had pretty much forgotten about Eddie moving out and Ma pressuring me to finish the college application. The fog had lifted, the sun was warm on my back, and my arms ached in a good way. Lobster boats crisscrossed the bay with fishermen tending their traps. All I had left to do was fish the traps in the Narrows, which were sure to be full, the way my luck had been running.

But all those good feelings faded when I came around the point on Indigo Island, looked up the Narrows, and saw the surface of the water. It was just an empty reflection of the sky. I searched the Narrows for my green-and-orange buoys, looking just under the surface in case they had shifted to deeper water. Nothing. Not a single buoy where yesterday there were ten.

Chapter 4

I came into Tate's wharf a little hard, thudding against the dock. Gulls circled and screeched overhead.

"Where the hell'd you learn to pilot a boat?"

It was Roger. He let out a rough laugh. Roger, Richard Grimes, and Bobby Nuckles were in the shade of an old toolshed among coils of rope, broken traps waiting to be repaired, and a barrel of rotting fish. I had enough problems on my mind without having to deal with them, so I pretended that I hadn't heard Roger.

I tied off my boat and heaved a crate of lobsters onto the wharf. Darrell Tate was at the end of the dock helping lower a barrel of bait into Joe Coleman's lobster boat. Darrell's bald head was turning red from the effort. A screen door slammed shut, and I looked up to see Sonny Tate back out of the front door of the shop, dragging a pallet full of ice, lobsters, and crab across to the loading dock. She stood, turned, and wiped her forehead. I gave her a wave, and she nodded in return. Then she wiped her hands on her jeans and dragged the pallet the rest of the way across the loading dock and into the back of a waiting truck. After she pulled the back of the truck down, she leapt off the loading platform, and her long legs brought her down the wharf toward me.

Sonny and I were in the same grade at school and had a few classes together. She was Myron Tate's daughter and had been working at the dock about as long as I'd been lobstering on my own. Sonny knew her way around the wharf as well as anyone, but a few of the guys still gave her a hard time. Myron had her cleaning the wharf, pumping gas for the boats, and running errands for whoever needed them. This summer, with Myron in and out of the hospital with some kind of heart problem, Sonny, along with her uncle Darrell, practically ran the place day to day. Some of the guys said Myron was crazy to let her do so much, but they were just seeing her skinny arms and the freckles that dusted her nose. She had thick black hair that she tried to keep under control with an old baseball cap. And she had a lopsided smile and a crackly voice that reminded me of a seabird. There was something about Sonny, maybe the way she'd look anyone straight in the eye, that told you she could handle just about anything that came along. But all the guys saw was a girl.

"I've got a crate of lobsters for you, Sonny," I said. "Where do you want them?"

"Let's weigh them and take them up to the shop," she said, taking one end of the crate. I took the other end, and we started walking up the wharf with the lobsters between us.

"I had a feeling the fog wouldn't keep you from going out today," she said.

"It wasn't so bad," I said. "The fog's lifted."

Sonny glanced at the hazy sky. "I don't know," she said. "We might have this stuff for a while."

We set the lobsters on a scale, and Sonny noted the weight on a clipboard. I'd be paid at the end of the week for what I brought in.

We went up the steps and into the shop, which wasn't much more than a shed with cedar shingles slapped on the side and a fading sign above the door that read "Tate's Lobster Co." Inside a couple bare light bulbs hung from the ceiling. The walls were rough pine, the floor cracked cement. The air was damp and smelled like a mixture of salt, fish, and sand. It wasn't a bad smell. The shop was mostly an office with invoices and other papers scattered across a big desk. A door in the back led to a supply room and a walk-in cooler where bait was kept.

"Let's leave them here," Sonny said. "I'll take care of them."

We set the crate next to a slate tank full of lobsters. Fresh seawater ran into the tank through a plastic hose. They were for people who came down to the wharf to find their dinner that night. The lobsters waiting to be shipped out wholesale were kept in floating pens at the end of the wharf.

It's funny how these lobsters go from our bay all over the world. We haul them off the seabed, where they've been crawling around looking for food to eat, and then they're airfreighted to New York City, to California, to France, to Japan—everywhere. The lobsters I catch probably see more of the world than I ever will. Which is fine with me.

In the corner of the room, I noticed a wet suit and a scuba tank. "Whose gear is that?" I asked.

"Mine," Sonny said.

"I didn't know you dove."

"I learned over the winter."

"Do you like it?" I couldn't imagine going scuba diving.

"It's great," Sonny said, pointing out the window at the bay. "You look at that ocean, gray and cold, and you wouldn't know there's all that life down there. It's another world. We ought to go sometime."

"I don't think so," I said, trying to laugh. "I like it better on top of the water. You know, where you can breathe if you want to."

Sonny started placing the lobsters in the tank, where they scuttled around and scratched against the slate. "For someone who likes lobstering so much, I'd think you'd want to see where they lived."

"Thanks for the offer. I'll let you know if I change my mind." I left the shop and headed for my boat. At the bottom of the steps a pebble hit me on the leg.

"Nice shot," someone said. It was Roger. "Hey, Dain, come over here. We want to talk with you."

I didn't want to talk with him, but with Roger it was better to do what he said. I was always quiet when he was around, hoping he wouldn't notice me. But this time I didn't have a choice, so I walked over slowly, like I was dragging lead weights.

Roger, Richard, and Bobby were still hunkered in the shade of the toolshed. Richard spat chewing tobacco onto the ground, and Bobby puffed on a cigarette. His foot jerked around nervously, like a hooked mackerel at the end of a line. He was always jumpy. Way too jumpy. And Roger, he was just looking at the horizon as calm as could be. I waited for a minute, a long, long minute, before he said anything.

"So, how's the fishing?" he asked in a friendly tone.

"Not bad," I said.

"Haven't got yourself tangled up in anyone else's line, have you?" He turned to Richard and Bobby. "You should have seen him squirming around trying to get that rope free yesterday. A regular minnow he was."

Richard and Bobby chuckled. I could feel my face turning red. I wanted to walk away, but I was too scared to move.

"No," I said. "No problems."

"Didn't lose any traps recently?" Roger asked.

"Yeah, today. I lost a few in the Narrows."

"In the Narrows. That's funny. What do you think happened to them? Tide get 'em?" Roger picked up a slat from a broken trap and began drawing in the dirt.

"Someone cut them. That's what happened." The boldness of my answer surprised me and made me nervous. But Roger was talking about my traps, and I wasn't going to hold back, even to him.

"Now, why would somebody go and do a thing like that?" He was acting dumb. I went along with it. I didn't have any choice, really.

"I don't know."

"Well, maybe they were sending a message."

"Maybe."

"People do that sometimes, send little messages. You know, like keep them traps out of the Narrows, or else . . ." Roger poked at a raggedy old cat that was nosing around the barrel of fish. It ran off a few feet but circled back, attracted by the irresistible smell of rotten fish.

"Or else what?"

"Usually, with these people sending messages, it's or else something worse will come your way. You just never know." Roger grinned like he was telling the best joke in the world. "But it could have been the tide that got them. Who knows?"

"Hey, Dain, you want the money now?" It was Sonny calling from the front porch. She didn't owe me any money. She was just trying to give me an excuse to get out of there.

"Well, looky here," Roger said, staring at Sonny. He jabbed the slat into the barrel of fish, sending a cloud of buzzing flies into the air. He pulled out a monkfish, its dried skin pulled back, exposing a mouth full of jagged teeth. "Sonny, why don't you come over here and give this poor old fish some mouth-to-mouth resuscitation?"

Richard and Bobby busted up. "Yeah, why don't you give us all some mouth-to-mouth?" Bobby said.

I could feel my teeth grinding. I wanted to tell them to shut up, but instead I stood there silently, waiting for the scene to end.

"I don't think mouth-to-mouth works on weasels," Sonny said, leaning on the porch railing. "Best thing is to hit them over the head till they start breathing again."

Bobby and Richard's laughter petered out. "Weasels," Bobby muttered. "That's real funny."

"It made me laugh," said a voice. I looked over and was relieved to see Eddie leaning against the side of the shop. I wondered how long he had been listening.

"Well, look who's here," Roger said. "It's Dain's big, bad brother, come just in time to save the day."

"Cut the crap, Roger."

"Sure, Eddie."

"Dain, come over here," Eddie said. "I want to talk to you."

Sonny went back inside, and I followed Eddie to the parking lot.

"What was that all about?" he asked.

"Nothing."

"So what's going on?"

"I think somebody cut some of my traps," I said, looking back at Roger, who had skewered several fish on the slats and stuck them in the ground.

"So what're you going to do?"

"I'm not sure."

"Is that what you were talking to Roger about?"

"Yeah."

"What did he say?"

"Basically, he said to get out of the Narrows."

"You might want to take his advice."

I didn't say anything. I studied Eddie as he shook a cigarette out of a pack and lit it. He had the moves down pat. I didn't even know he smoked.

"Why do you hang around with Roger?" I asked.

"Oh, I don't know. We get along. He's not that bad."

"Whatever." I didn't want to hear about it. I picked up a rock and hurled it at an oil drum. It sailed wide.

"So what do you think I should do?" I asked.

"About?"

"The Narrows."

"Get out."

"You think?"

"Definitely."

I shook my head. "You're the one who told me I had to learn to stand up for myself."

"Did I say that?"

"Yeah, you did."

"Well, sometimes it's better to stay out of the way of trouble."

"Yeah? Like you do?"

Eddie gave me a hard look. "I ain't perfect," he said. "And I'm not telling you what to do. You can figure it out for yourself."

I stalked back to my boat and watched Eddie join Roger by the shed. Roger slapped him on the back and said something I didn't catch. Eddie laughed. I untied my boat and took her across the bay as fast as I could.

I throttled back on the engine, passing the southern point of Trimble Island. Perched on rocks along the shore and circling in the air, gulls and cormorants bickered and fought.

It seemed like the whole world wanted me to quit lobstering. Ma. Roger. Even Eddie. Brother, if it came to a lobster war, Roger would blow me off the water. Who did I have on my side? No one. I couldn't even count on Eddie anymore.

Chapter 5

Ma was bent over the flower bed on the sunny side of our house, a pair of cutting shears in her hand. She was working on a rosebush with a dozen blood-red flowers in full bloom. If the weather was good, like it was that afternoon, you'd find her in the garden weeding and watering, plucking the dead leaves and snipping the flowers. The garden responded to her and grew. It grew in the beds, up the trellises, and spilled over the pots. I think she liked to spend time there because it was about the one thing she knew she could protect.

She waved me over. She wore jeans and a baseball hat to keep the sun off her light skin. She was always rubbing lotions on her skin: sun protector, skin softener, and wrinkle remover.

"Your uncle wants to talk to you," Ma said, fanning herself with her hat.

"He does?"

"Said you should drop by."

"What does he want to talk about?"

"I'm not sure. He didn't say."

My mother thought she was clever, that I wouldn't see through her. She probably called Uncle Ray earlier and told him she was worried about me and that I needed a good talking to from a man. I liked Uncle Ray, so I didn't mind too much. He tried to look out for Eddie and me after Dad died.

"Okay," I said. "I'll drop by."

Ma hesitated for a moment. "You haven't seen Eddie, have you?"

I paused and thought about telling her about my traps getting cut and about Eddie and Roger at the dock. But I caught a hopeful look in her eyes and decided to keep quiet. It would only upset her, and what could she tell me, anyway? "No, Ma. I haven't."

She looked at the dirt on her hands for a moment. "Okay, Dain. Don't forget about your uncle."

"I'll go now," I said.

Uncle Ray lived about two miles away through the woods. Honey ran ahead of me, her nose to the ground, as we cut across the field behind our house. She leapt over the stone wall that separated the field from the trees, and then I followed her into the woods.

I stopped for a moment, leaning against an oak, and let my eyes adjust to the dark. Besides the chatter of red squirrels in the treetops I could hear a buzzing noise. I wasn't sure if it was the mosquitoes or the thoughts racing through my head. I set off along an old trail that ran through the woods, parallel to the shore. In the distance, I could hear Honey crashing through the underbrush.

After I had walked about twenty minutes, I came to an outcrop that overlooked the bay. The smell of pine needles mixed with the saltiness of the sea, which spread all around, glittering blue. A sailboat cut across the bay, its white sails blown full by the wind.

I lay back on a bed of moss and stared at the sky through a maze of branches. They were as tangled as my thoughts, and I could hardly keep my feelings straight. Should I set my traps again? Should I get ready to go to college like Ma wanted? And Eddie, what was happening to him? I felt like I was caught in the surf, not sure which way was up. Life wasn't always this confusing. In the old days, when Dad was still here, everything made sense, and we watched out for each other.

I remembered the first time I went lobstering. I must have been about four years old and Eddie seven. I was so excited to go out with Eddie, my dad, and Uncle Ray that I hardly slept the night before. I even remember the first lobster we caught that day.

Eddie and I peered into the water, our hands tightly gripping the side of the boat, waiting for the first trap to come up from the seabed. I was about ready to jump out of my skin when we finally saw the outlines of the trap rising through the dark, green water. The winch pulled it out of the sea with a *sploosh*, water cascading from the sides. There was a starfish stuck to the side, and barnacles and algae. It looked like it had been at the bottom of the sea for a million years.

Uncle Ray swung the trap over to the side where Eddie and I had been leaning. He opened the trap and fished around until he pulled out a lobster. The lobster waved its jagged claws. I took a step back.

Uncle Ray showed me and Eddie how to hold it. Eddie took the lobster by its back and brought it right to his face to look at closely. "You hold it," he said.

Slowly, I took the lobster from Eddie, holding on as tight as I could. He let go, and it was all mine.

I remember Dad saying, "Your first lobster."

Eddie and I smiled at each other.

I remember the salt spray stung my eyes. I leaned over the side of the boat anyway, watching the waves hit the bow and cut off in arcs.

Eddie was at my elbow. He was looking out to sea, at the islands as we went by, at the buoys and the birds. Light bounced off the tips of the waves, sliding this way and that. The second I stared at one spot, at one wave, it changed, disappeared, or shifted. The water wouldn't stay still. I leaned over the side of the boat to try to touch the water. I thought I could touch one of those warm spots of light in the moment it flashed. I leaned farther. I could hear Dad and Uncle Ray's comforting chatter as they steered.

My fingers were so close to the light, and then there was a flash at the tip of a wave, and I grabbed for it, and I knew I had it in my hand, and then I felt a lurch as the boat rocked to the side. I lost my balance and was suddenly in the cold, cold water, way over my head.

Salt water filled my mouth, and I spluttered. I saw blue sky. A gull. I barely knew how to swim, but I could feel the life vest holding me up. Where was the side of the boat? Miles away? That's how it felt, because I thought I'd been in the water for just about forever. That's how surprised I was. No. The boat was just a little farther on. I saw Eddie climb onto the edge of the boat. His legs kicked out as he went over, his arms in the air. His hair blew back as he and his orange life vest went down into the water.

By the time Eddie got to me, the gull had flown away and Dad had pulled the boat around. Eddie had a hand on my vest. I wasn't going anywhere.

The boat eased alongside us. Uncle Ray pulled me up with one hand and Eddie with the other, like we were pieces of driftwood, light as can be.

"Look what I got," he said. "A couple of sea monsters."

"Throw 'em back in," Dad said. "Nobody wants any sea monsters. They're too ugly to eat."

I started laughing. Eddie was laughing, too.

That's how I remembered it. That's how it was going to be. My dad and his brother. Me and Eddie. Out on the water lobstering, working hard and laughing. All that laughing.

Honey nudged my arm. It was time to get moving. I stood up and brushed pine needles off my clothes, wishing things could be like before. Out on the bay, the fog was starting to creep across the water.

By the time I came out of the woods, dusk was falling and the bats were coming out, dipping through the sky. Honey trotted at my side, her tail brushing my leg as we walked down Uncle Ray's driveway. His house was set way back off the main road, surrounded by the woods. It was a small house, one-and-a-half stories, with weathered cedar shingles on the side. Perfect for an old bachelor, Uncle Ray always said. It belonged to a state college, which used it as a marine biology research station. Uncle Ray made sure the buildings on the property were painted, the boats were taken up in the winter, and the roofs didn't leak. The summers were busy with keeping the boats running and the lawns mowed. In the winter, Uncle Ray plowed driveways, and if there wasn't any snow, he sat around the wood stove smoking his pipe and telling stories to whoever would listen—his old cronies, college students, or me.

When I reached the house, it looked like nobody was home. The lights were off, and it was quiet, except for some crickets chirping in the grass. Then I saw the glow of Uncle Ray's pipe on the screened-in porch.

"Howdy, Dain," he called out.

"Hi, Uncle," I said, climbing the steps. Uncle Ray sat in a chair with his pipe in his plate-sized hand. Even in the dark you could tell he had a fisherman's face—wrinkles from the sun and wind crossed his cheeks, ran over his mouth, and lined his forehead. He had fished his whole life, until the day Dad drowned. That was the end of it for him.

"Have a seat," he said, pointing with his pipe to the other chair. "Something to drink?"

"Sure."

He poured me a glass of iced tea from a pitcher. I took a gulp. It was sweet and filled with fresh mint from his garden.

"So, what's up?" I asked.

"You tell me," he said, relighting his pipe.

"Not much."

"I heard you were having a problem with your traps."

"How'd you hear about that?"

He chuckled. "It's a small town, Dain."

"Well, it's no problem."

"You didn't lose some traps?"

"Yeah, a few. You know the current in the Narrows."

"Sure, it runs pretty strong."

"I guess it took them into deeper water. I'll find those traps. Don't worry about me—I can handle it."

"It sounds like somebody was just telling me a story, then. You know how people get when they've got time on their hands. Their imaginations start up, just to keep things interesting."

"They must have been pretty bored if that's what they were telling you."

"Well, that's what I thought, but I figured I'd better check it out."

"So that's what you wanted to see me about?"

"Not exactly," he said, tapping his pipe on an ashtray. "Your mom tells me she found that college application I gave you in a garbage can. How'd it end up there?"

"I guess I put it there."

"Now, why'd you go and do that? Don't you want to go to college? You do good in school."

"I do okay."

"Better than we ever did." Uncle Ray smiled.

"I don't see the need."

He leaned forward to look me closer in the face. "You don't see the need?"

"You and Dad didn't go."

"No, but we would have. It just wasn't in the cards for us."

"I want to be a lobsterman like Dad," I said.

"So you can go around getting your traps cut?" He hit the table with his hand, and a cloud of ashes fell on the floor. "You want to live like that?"

"It was the tide," I said.

"Sure it was."

Uncle Ray stood abruptly and looked out through the screen across the dark lawn. He shook his head and ran his hand through his gray hair. He stood that way for almost a minute. I began to think he had forgotten that I was even there.

"Dain, you're still young. You've got choices," he finally said. He sounded tired. "Your dad and me, we were just trying to make ends meet. We were pushing our luck. We thought we could beat that storm. Well, we couldn't. Learned my lesson too late. Some things you just can't beat. It catches up to you."

He put his big hand to the screen, touching it gently like it was a fine netting that might break. "I don't need to tell you about it," he said. "You know already."

It was the first time I had ever heard Uncle Ray say one word about that day. But I knew the story. A storm was starting to kick up. Only a couple other boats tried going out that morning, and they turned right around before leaving the harbor. Dad and Uncle Ray kept going though.

They had just reached their first string and, right there, with swells rolling and waves crashing into the ledge around Trimble Island, Dad got tangled in his gear. In a split second, the rope wrapped around his leg and yanked him overboard and pulled him under. Uncle Ray fought the wind and rain to bring the boat around and get the rope back, but by the time he reached him, it was too late. He brought my father back, lying on the deck of the boat while the rain beat down. Ma said Uncle Ray blamed himself, but there was no one to blame. It was just the ocean.

A June bug smashed against the screen. I put my glass on the table and watched a drop of water run down the side.

"Come on," Uncle Ray said. "I want to show you something."

We went outside and across the lawn toward the shore. Honey crawled out from under the porch and tagged along at our heels. Down by the dock, where the college kept a couple boats, there was a large shingled lab building. Uncle Ray took out a set of keys on a chain and unlocked the door. It was dark inside except for the glow of aquarium lights. There were a dozen tanks in a row. Water gurgled through pipes and filters.

"You'll like this," he said, bending down to look into one of the tanks.

Inside was a mass of starfish wriggling their long legs and a group of sea anemones, brown and red, waving their tentacles in the current from a filter. Several sea cucumbers, looking like bruised, bumpy sausages, were stuck to the glass. Uncle Ray tapped the side of the tank with his pipe.

"Where's this stuff from?" I asked.

"Out in the bay."

"From our bay?" I shivered.

Uncle Ray laughed. "See? There's more out there than even you know about."

I looked into another tank. It was dark. There were some rocks piled in the back, and I leaned closer to see what was behind them. Suddenly, a giant mouth full of teeth erupted from the rocks. I jumped back.

Uncle Ray laughed again. "Surprised you, eh? She's a mean old bugger."

It was the ugliest fish I had ever seen, with mottled skin, bulging eyes, and a monstrous mouth.

"You could study marine biology," Uncle Ray said.

"Maybe."

"You know lots about it already. More than some of the knuckleheads that come through here. Half of them don't know the difference between a shag and a shearwater."

The fish with the teeth swam back and forth at the front of the tank like it wanted to get out and swim away.

"Dain, all I'm trying to say is that you're lucky. You've got choices. You can lobster if you want. You can go to college. It's not like one rules out the other. Anyway, you know what your mother thinks about it."

"Yeah, I know." I pictured all those college catalogs stuffed into a drawer in my room. It was clear what Ma wanted.

"Course, what matters is what you think."

I followed Uncle Ray past the tanks and back outside onto the lawn where Honey was waiting for us. In the still night air we could hear the sound of waves rolling against the shore. Uncle Ray put his arm on my shoulder. "I know you'll do the right thing, Dain."

It was dark, so I'm sure Uncle Ray couldn't see the doubt on my face.

Chapter 6

The next morning the fog was thicker than the day before, blotting out the sun so you'd almost forget it was day. I took my time getting around the bay, listening to my internal radar, looking out for ledges and rocks. In fog like that, you had to practically run over your buoys to find them. I didn't miss a trap.

I thought about what Uncle Ray had said—about how he and my father had been pushing their luck, about those "choices" I had—but, like I said before, lobstering made sense to me, and the beginnings of a decision I had made in bed waiting to go to sleep became clearer and clearer. I wasn't going to let anybody or anything push me off the water, not the current, not my family, not Roger Gribbin, nobody. Lobstering was something I could do well, and it was a connection I had to my father. He had been a good lobsterman, and I was sure he would have wanted me to be one, too.

I motored through the fog, moving from string to string, my senses alert. When I got to the Narrows, I set some more traps where mine had got lost, and then I headed for Tate's wharf to see if I could find Eddie. I wanted to tell him about resetting my traps, and I needed to talk to him about going to college. It was like the old days: I needed him to listen.

It was quiet at the wharf. Sonny was inside sweeping, Isaac Fuller was tying up his skiff at the dock, and the fog kept rolling in. I was just hanging around with my hands in my pockets waiting to see if Eddie would come by. Arnie Cater stood next to me, smoking a cigarette he had carefully rolled with his knobby fingers. He had his flatbed parked on the wharf, a stack of wire lobster traps on the back.

We watched Isaac tuck his oars away and lift a bucket onto the dock. He stood bent over, like he was leaning into the wind. His wiry brown hair looked like a mat of seaweed drying on the beach. He had a beard thick and long enough to hide a couple of herons. Grabbing the bucket, he pulled himself up the gangway, which was steep with the low tide.

"Arnie, how are you?" he panted.

"I'm mad." Arnie rested one hand on his hip, just above his low-slung jeans.

"What happened?"

"Some sons of bitches stole my crates."

"That's bad."

"I left them at the end of the dock, and someone stole them."

"Now, who'd do that?" They both looked at me, as if I might know something about it, as if I'd have an explanation for how someone could steal some lobster traps. I shrugged, hoping to show that I thought only a real low-down person would have stolen Arnie's traps.

"Kids probably. If I find out who's got them, they're in for it." Arnie waved his hands in the air.

"Could have us a real old-fashioned lobster war," Isaac said with a hopeful flash in his eyes.

"That's right," Arnie said. "We could show those kids what it's really like. Teach them not to mess with us old geezers, ha! They wouldn't know what hit 'em, would they?"

"It's been awhile, eh?" Isaac said.

"There ain't been a real lobster war since Stanley Wiggins laid a string of traps off Brindle Point," Arnie said. "Thinking Mike Allard wouldn't care. Hee hee. He shouldn't've done that."

"No, suh," Isaac said. "Before that summer was over the Wiggins, cousins and all, were having it out with Mike and the rest of his family. You know they've got family all over the bay."

"I think between it all, they lost about a hundred strings of traps, three boats, and a marriage," Arnie said. "You remember that?"

"Who could forget?"

"No one talks about it now, but back then, for that one summer there was all hell out on the water," Arnie said.

Sonny came out to see what was going on. She held the broom in her hand. I nodded hey to her, but the men didn't pay her any attention.

Then Arnie peered in Isaac's bucket. "Say, what you got there?" he asked, nudging it with his boot.

"I don't know," Isaac said.

The fish barely fit in the bucket. Isaac tipped it out onto the dock. It was flat, with wings almost two feet wide, a tail pointed like an arrow, and two black, staring eyes.

"You weren't taking any chances," Arnie said, pointing to a gash on the fish's head.

"Oh no, I made sure it was good and dead," Isaac replied.

"Looks like a skate," Sonny said, rolling the sleeves of her flannel shirt up to her elbows.

"A skate? So that's a stinger it's got in the tail. I could've been stung!"

"No, that's a ray you're thinking of," Sonny told him. "A skate just looks bad, but it won't hurt you. Where'd you get it?"

"I was fishing for flounder by Alder Creek."

"Alder Creek? You were fishing out there in this fog? You didn't get any, did you?" Arnie asked.

"Naw."

"You won't get any flounder there, anyway," Sonny said. "The bottom's all rocky. Flounder like sand or mud that they can rake through looking for food."

"How do you know what the bottom's like there?" I asked.

"I've been diving there," she said. "I've seen it."

We all looked at the skate like it might just float up into the air and fly away.

"Well, at least you got a skate," I said.

"Yeah." Isaac scratched his beard. "But it ain't no good for anything, is it?"

"Nope," said Arnie.

Isaac nudged the skate with his foot to the edge of the wharf and let it plop into the water. It turned upside down, and we watched the white belly disappear as it sank to the bottom.

"What are you fellows looking at?" We turned around. A man stood next to a station wagon with state plates. He wore jeans and a khaki shirt with a Marine Resources patch on the shoulder. He had some papers in one hand and a hammer in the other. He came over to where the four of us were standing and looked into the water where Isaac had dumped the skate. Then he studied the fog for a minute. "Boy, you can't see much on a day like this, can you?" he said.

"Not a lot," Isaac replied.

"I'm Brad Simpson. Marine Resources."

"We can see that," Isaac said, eyeing the sheets of paper in his hand.

"Oh, these," Simpson said. "They've got me putting up notices. Can't go out today, so they give me this."

"Notices?" Arnie said.

"Sure, for the meeting."

We looked at him blankly.

"The fisheries hearings," he said.

Sonny nodded. "Sure, we've heard about them. Talking about the lobster stocks. How they're doing."

"That's right," Simpson said. "We're holding the meetings up and down the coast so we can get some input into how things are going. How the stocks are looking. If we need to do anything more to protect them."

Arnie grimaced. "Seems like you're doing more than enough," he muttered.

"It's just to get more information," Simpson said. "Make sure everyone's working together. Nothing to get worried about."

He turned on his heel, tacked a notice to the bulletin board next to the door of the shop, and hopped into his car. We watched his red taillights fade into the mist.

Isaac and Arnie frowned. "The state's coming in," Isaac said. "They're going to run the show."

"That's right," Arnie said. "They know better than we do."

"There's tons of lobsters," I said. "They're everywhere."

Arnie and Isaac scowled. I glanced at Sonny, hoping to see what she was thinking, but just then the phone started ringing in the shop, and she ran to get it.

Sonny's sudden action seemed to break a spell. Arnie jumped into his truck and pulled out. Isaac scuttled down the gangway, untied his boat, and set out across the water.

I went into the shop to talk to Sonny. On the desk, next to a tattered book of marine charts, were several college brochures and applications, just like the ones my mother had been collecting for me. I thought about it for a moment and decided that it made sense for Sonny to go to college. She was smart. She could do about anything she wanted.

I looked up. Sonny was off the phone, staring out the window at the fog.

"Are you okay?" I asked.

She jerked her head like she had forgotten where she was. "It was my mother. They took my dad back to the hospital for more tests today, and they found something they don't understand. They want him to stay overnight."

Before I could say anything, Sonny started neatening the desk, like she had to be doing something. She gathered some loose papers into a pile, which burst from her hands and fluttered to the floor.

She shook her head. "I'm a mess," she said.

I bent down to pick up the papers. "They're just being safe," I said. "They have good doctors at the hospital."

"I know," Sonny said.

I handed the papers to her. "It'll be all right."

She didn't answer. She had already turned away and was looking into the fog again.

On the way home, I spotted Eddie in my rearview mirror. He was in his truck. I put on my blinker and started to pull onto the shoulder. But instead of slowing down, Eddie roared by me, his hair blowing crazily in the wind. He didn't even glance at me when I waved at him to pull over. I tried to speed up and catch him, but he was accelerating fast and my old truck started to shudder when I hit fifty-five. I blinked my lights to try to get him to stop, but I guess he didn't see me, and he kept going faster until he disappeared around the curve. When I got to the bend, he was out of sight. I hit my steering wheel with my fists. So much for my luck changing.

I pulled in at Hoppin's General Store to get a soda. The paint outside was peeling in big patches and the roof over the porch sagged. Two gas pumps, one faded red, the other aquamarine, stood on an island with a bucket of soapy water between them for cleaning windshields. Only Walter's car was in the parking lot. A bell tinkled when I pushed the screen door open.

Walter Hoppin sat on a stool behind the register sorting candy into jars, dropping them in one by one with his pudgy hands. He had a round face and crossed eyes that floated in their sockets. Tufts of hair stuck out of his ears. He looked like a deep-sea fish that's never seen the light.

"How's it going, Walter?"

He lifted his head, caught my gaze, and blinked slowly several times. Then he swiveled around and stared out the window. The fog was hanging low over the trees, not settling, but not lifting, either. The sun was barely getting through. He swung his head back around, and one of his eyes fixed on me.

"Not so good," he grumbled. "Been real slow. All this fog, it's keeping the tourists away. August should be my best month."

I spun a creaky rack of faded postcards. They were blurry and curled at the corners. Even in the best of times, Walter didn't see too many tourists in his store.

The door banged open with a crack, giving Walter a start, and Roger Gribbin stomped in. He gave us a brief glance, then strode by the cold cuts and pickles, the stand of potato chips and the rack of bread, and went directly to the wall-to-wall refrigerator at the back of the store. He looked the selection up and down, took out a case of beer, and then two more. He carried them to the front without straining at the weight of all those full cans and dropped them on the counter, sending a pile of sourballs across the floor.

"Looks like someone's having a party," Walter said, stooping to pick up a few sourballs.

"That's right, Walter. A little celebration," Roger said, flashing his wallet open. He had a bunch of tens and twenties in it—new, crisp bills. "Throw in ten lotto tickets while you're at it."

Walter peeled off the lottery tickets. Roger wasn't twenty-one, but Walter wasn't going to say anything. Roger had been buying beer there for years. What was Walter going to do except hope that the police didn't catch him? He slowly rang up the bill, carefully depressing the keys on the register as if it was a machine he was using for the first time.

"Oh boy, we're going to let it rip tonight," Roger said, rubbing my head like I was a dog. "You should come by, Dain. I'm sure Eddie will be in fine form."

"He'll be there?" I said.

"Eddie? Are you kidding? He lives there, remember? Anyway, Eddie wouldn't miss a party. You really should see him after he's had a few. The life of the party!"

Roger picked up the beer, laughed to himself, and left. The screen door thwacked shut behind him, leaving Walter and me in the stillness of the store. It was like we were in water that was beginning to settle after a shark had come thrashing through.

Walter shook his head and sighed. "Those boys, they sure have got a head for trouble," he said. "Nothing but trouble."

Chapter 7

Trees leaned over the dirt road, their branches scraping the side of my truck. Fog hovered overhead in the darkness. Everything seemed to be pressing in on me, but I kept on going up that roadway, through those woods. At the end of the road was Emmit Gribbin's farmhouse, and behind the farmhouse was Roger Gribbin's trailer, where I hoped I'd find Eddie.

Finally, the woods opened out into a field. An old hay baler and a rusty tractor stood at the edge, ready to turn the grass into hay.

At the top of the field, my headlights flashed across the Gribbins' house, which sat on a rise. It was unpainted, the shutters askew, and a pair of cat eyes blinked from an upstairs window. A black dog at the end of its chain bared its teeth and growled at my truck as I passed by, still following the road, which curved to the side of the house and around the barn. Behind the house was more field, and at the back of the field was Roger's trailer, light slashing out from the open windows, cutting into the mist.

I parked with the other cars and trucks in the field and sat for a moment listening to the sounds of the party: music and laughing and hubbub. I licked my hand and tried brushing back my hair, looking in the rearview mirror. A kid stared back.

I closed my eyes. Eddie wouldn't hesitate for a second. He'd go right on in. I opened my eyes and got out of the truck. Smoothing out my shirt, I marched over to the trailer, climbed the front steps, and stood at the door. I was about to knock, but that was stupid. I had to go straight in, like a guy in a movie, just like Eddie would.

As I stood on the cinder-block steps, trying to talk myself into going inside, the door flew open and Mike Keller, all one hundred and eighty pounds of him, lurched out. I barely got out of his way. He stumbled across the gravel drive, went straight through some bushes, and climbed into his flatbed truck. The engine sparked, and he wheeled the truck back, spinning the tires in the gravel. Then he peeled out and went up the road so fast that a couple of lobster traps fell off the back. A few seconds later, after the sound of Mike's truck faded, I took a breath, pulled open the screen door, and went on in.

For a minute, nobody noticed me. The air was hot and filled with smoke. The stereo was cranked. I didn't recognize anyone at first in the press of tangled bodies. Beer bottles and cans sat on the tables, floor, and window sills. Then I saw Bobby Nuckles, his mouth open wide as he laughed. Next to him Richard Grimes leaned in a doorway, his eyes as thin as slits. Roger was on the couch with his feet on the coffee table. Tina Branscombe sat next to him playing with her bracelet. Roger wasn't talking to anyone. He looked like he was a million miles away, ignoring the smoke and music and chatter that swirled all around him.

"I ain't seen anything like it," Bobby said.

"Like what?" Richard asked.

"This fog. I don't remember any fog in August like this. It's weird. It's driving my dogs crazy. They bark all night and sleep all day. Can't get any sleep myself."

"You're right," Richard said. "It is weird."

The conversations around Richard and Bobby had come to a lull while everyone thought about the fog and how it was kind of spooky. Still, nobody had noticed me standing at the door with my hands in my back pockets, trying to pretend that I fit right in.

"When do you think it'll lift?" Richard asked.

"The weathermen say in a couple days," Bobby said.

"The *weathermen?*" Richard said. "What do they know?"

"I don't think it's ever going to lift," Roger told the room in a booming voice. "It'll just stay like this. Forever."

Richard, Bobby, and Tina turned and stared at Roger.

"Forever?" Richard said, not sure if Roger was serious or joking.

"Yeah. Forever."

"You're nuts," Richard said. "You know that? Completely nuts."

Roger just grinned. The thing about Roger was that nobody was about to mess with him, even just talking about the weather. Someone started to chuckle, and then in a second everyone was laughing. "If it ain't never gonna lift," Bobby said, "we'd better get some more beer!"

The chatter picked up again, and everyone turned to talk to whoever was next to them. I didn't see Eddie anywhere. Then I noticed that Tina was looking at me. She nudged Roger and pointed.

Roger smiled. "It's Eddie's little brother," he said, waving me over and pushing Tina out of her seat.

"Nice of you to come," Roger said when I sat down.

"Seen Eddie?" I asked.

Roger picked up a snow globe from the table and didn't answer. It was a present that I had given Eddie after a class trip to Boston.

"Like it?" Roger asked. He held it up to the light and shook it. A snowstorm erupted inside the glass, swirling around a sailboat. The boat disappeared. I held my breath, waiting for the boat to come back into view. Slowly, the snowflakes settled, and I could breathe again.

Roger put the snow globe back on the table. "Hey, somebody get the kid a beer," he yelled. In a minute, Tina put a cold bottle in my hand.

"You do drink beer, don't you?" Roger asked.

"Sure." I had had a few at Uncle Ray's, but I don't think I finished any of them. They were too bitter, and the smell nearly made me gag. But I took a sip of the beer Tina gave me and forced it down.

"It's nice you could come by and be friendly," Roger said.

"I was looking for Eddie."

"For Eddie? Well, let's see. Last I saw him, he was with Shirley Timilty. You know Shirley, don't you? I think she's got a thing for your brother. Boy, you can't keep the girls off of him."

He looked me over. "You have a girlfriend yet? Maybe that Sonny Tate?"

I didn't bother answering. He put his arm over my shoulder like we were pals. "Don't worry about it," he said. "Women aren't all they're cracked up to be."

I took another sip from my beer, trying not to think about Roger's arm, with its snarl of tattoos, weighing on my back.

"That's the spirit," Roger said, squeezing my shoulder hard. "Drink up." He drained his beer, setting the empty can on the floor. Then he turned and studied my face for a moment. A drop of sweat trickled down the side of my forehead. "Tell me, Dain, what's your philosophy in life?"

"Philosophy?" I asked, surprised.

"Sure. You've got to have a philosophy. Some people believe in God. Some people believe in money. It helps them make their decisions, get through the days."

"I don't think I have one," I said, startled that Roger would be talking like this to me.

"That's tough, Dain," he said. "You know what I think? I think there's no one in this world that's going to help you. You've got to take care of yourself. If you see something you want, something you need—you get it. Don't let anything stand in your way. 'Cause no one's going to help you, Dain. No one. Not even Eddie."

Roger's eyes narrowed, like they were boring into me. "What do you think of that?"

"I don't know," I said, wondering if he was right.

Roger was just about whispering now, and I had to lean close to hear him. "I know what you think," he said. "Don't think I don't. You don't like me. But I don't care. One thing you gotta remember, though, is Eddie, he's like me. Peas in a pod, that's what my grandma says. You think you know him, Dain, but you don't. You don't *really* know him. Not like I do."

I got up. Roger didn't know what he was talking about. I did know Eddie, and he wasn't like Roger at all. He wasn't mean. He wasn't angry. He wasn't crazy. "I'm going to find Eddie," I said.

"Okay," Roger said with a smile. "Take it easy on the girls, Dain. We don't want you getting in any trouble. And, Dain, don't worry about your mother. I won't tell her you were out drinking with the boys."

My mother. If she saw me here with a beer in my hand, hanging around Roger Gribbin and his friends, I knew exactly what she'd do. She wouldn't say a word, but her eyes would be speaking loud and clear: disappointment and total disapproval. Ma read the police reports faithfully. I knew the dry rustle of the newspaper and her heavy sigh. She was afraid that she'd find Eddie there, his crimes laid out in black and white for all the ladies at the church to read. She always let me know that so-and-so had been arrested by the police for operating without a license or driving drunk or being disorderly. When Ma let her imagination turn to Eddie, she disappeared down a long and dangerous tunnel.

I took a swig of beer and pushed my way toward the back of the trailer, tripping over legs that crossed the narrow hallway. No one seemed to mind. Cigarette smoke stung my eyes.

I glanced through a partly opened door leading to the bedroom. There were four guys inside sitting around a small table. They were playing cards, with bills and coins in the middle of the table and beer cans by their hands.

"Whatever you say about Roger, man, he knows how to treat his friends," one of them said. "Even when he's on the losing end of the cards."

"That's right," another said.

One of them saw me looking through the door. "Hey!" he said, shutting it before I could ask them about Eddie.

Then Tina stepped out of the bathroom. "Seen Eddie?" I asked, speaking over the music.

"I saw him twenty minutes ago," she said. "Said he was getting some air."

I stumbled outside and looked around. There was no sign of Eddie, but it felt good to be in the open air, away from all the people. I heard some voices coming from around the corner and walked toward the Gribbins' old poultry barn on the other side of the trailer. The lights were on, even though it looked like the barn hadn't been used in years. Sheets of corrugated tin were peeling off the side, and the roof sagged at the peak. A good winter storm could take the whole thing down in one blow.

As I listened, I heard Eddie's voice inside the barn. But mostly, it was a girl speaking. I strained to hear but couldn't catch the words. Then the barn door opened and a swath of light sprung across the ground. Someone stepped out, the door closed, and the light vanished. Shirley Timilty ran straight into me.

"Are you okay?" I asked.

"Who is it?" she said, wiping her eyes and not looking up.

"Me. Dain Harrington."

"Jesus, another Harrington. Are you as mixed up as your brother? He doesn't know what he wants!" Without another word, she stalked off and went into the party.

I crept up to the barn and rubbed a circle on the dusty window to look through. The glass was old and rippled, so I saw a wavering vision of hundreds of young chickens, maybe a month old, standing beneath heat lamps that hung from the rafters. Mr. Gribbin must have been trying to make some extra money on the side selling poultry.

Eddie was sprawled in the middle of the floor, a chicken pecking at his boot. He held a piece of newspaper in one hand and a beer in the other. He was intent on the words on the paper and seemed unaware of the chickens or anything else around him.

What was he doing on the floor of the Gribbins' poultry barn? Had he really made Shirley cry? Did Roger know him better than I did? I stumbled through the dark, groping for the door to the barn. I felt mist on the back of my neck and shivered.

The door creaked when I opened it. Warm, dry air hit my face, and the smell of sawdust and grain and chicken.

Eddie looked up from where he was sitting and folded the paper he had been reading. The lights cast long shadows on his face. Dust swirled through the lamplight like plankton in the sea. For a moment, in the silence of that barn, with the dark space in the rafters above and Eddie on the floor, I wanted to turn and walk away. There was something there that I didn't understand, something that scared me.

"Why don't you close the door, Dain. Raised in a barn?" Eddie smiled a loopy grin just like he used to, and I forgot about Roger leaning close and whispering in my ear, "You don't *really* know him." Overhead, an off-kilter fan turned slowly in a ventilation window. *Click, click, click.*

I shut the door and shuffled my way toward Eddie, scattering the chicks like Moses parting the sea.

"Have a seat," Eddie said.

I sat down, sweeping aside a few chicks. Eddie passed me his beer can. I took a gulp, trying not to wince as it went down.

"What're you doing, Eddie?"

"Getting some advice from my friends here. Gotta change my ways, these guys are telling me. Get on the straight and narrow. Boy, I never knew chickens were so smart. Real smart, these little guys. Yeah. Real smart."

"It looked like you were reading something," I said.

"Oh yeah. This." Eddie carefully handed me an article from a newspaper. I unfolded it. There was a picture of salmon running up a river and another of a trawler. The article was about fisheries in Alaska and the people who fished them. I folded the paper and gave it back. Eddie tucked it into his coat pocket.

"What's going on, Eddie? I saw Shirley outside. She didn't look too happy."

He ignored me and scooped up a chick. He held it close to his face, turning it from side to side to get a good look at it. He chirped at it and then set it down. I took another drink from the beer.

"There were some guys inside talking about Roger," I said. "They were playing cards. It looked like there was a lot of money on the table."

"You stay away from them," Eddie said sharply. "You stay clear away."

"Sure, Eddie. Sure," I said, wondering what I'd have to do with those guys, anyway. I'd probably never see them again.

Eddie took another drink of beer and was silent.

"Eddie?"

"Yeah?"

"We're friends, right?"

"Sure we're friends."

"You'd tell me anything, right?"

"Sure."

"Who's cutting my traps? Is it Roger?"

Eddie looked up into the rafters.

"If I knew what was going on, I might know what to do," I said. "I've got to find out who's cutting them."

"Why you gotta find out?"

"Because I have to know what I'm up against."

"What you're up against?"

"I reset those traps in the Narrows."

Eddie's eyes suddenly focused. "Why'd you do that? The season's about over. You have to go back to school. That's what you have to do. Get ready for college."

"You sound like Ma."

He laughed, his head rolling to the side. "Boy, she'd die to hear that. Me sounding like her."

"Well, I'm not going to any college," I said.

"So, what're you going to do?"

"Lobster."

"Just like Dad."

"Yeah, and just like you."

"Me?" Eddie asked, surprised.

"What's wrong with that? I wouldn't mind being like you."

"You don't want to be like me," Eddie barked. "You don't want to be anything like me."

"Yes, I do!" I said. He had no idea. I wanted to walk into a room full of people and not for a split second worry about what they were thinking of me. I wanted to be calm and easy, the way he was. That alone would have made half my worries go away.

"I ain't no hero, Dain."

"I know that," I said.

"Then why don't you get out of here and leave me alone," Eddie said. "You shouldn't be at this party, anyway. It's no place for you." He pulled another beer from his coat pocket, opened it, and took a gulp.

When I didn't move, he looked at me, and his eyes were wild and angry. "Beat it, Dain. Scram!"

I'd never seen Eddie like this before. I got up, spilling beer on my leg, and walked slowly to the door. I wanted to say something, but the words that came to my head were a garbled mess and didn't make any sense. I opened the door, paused, but never heard a word from Eddie. I stepped from the light into the foggy darkness and closed the door behind me.

Chapter 8

When I cracked open my eyes the next morning, I found Ma standing over my bed, her hands on her hips and a stone-cold expression on her face.

"I hope you had fun last night," she said.

I swung my legs out of bed. My jeans were still on.

"It smells like a brewery in here," she growled. "Cigarettes, too."

I pinched my eyes, trying to wake myself up so I could talk straight. I was on thin ice. How many beers did I drink? Enough to make me feel queasy.

"So what do you have to say for yourself?"

"Nothing."

"Where were you?"

"At a party."

"So while I was working, you were at a party. I sure hope it was good."

I shrugged and didn't answer.

"Whose party?"

"Roger's."

"Roger Gribbin?"

Ma opened her mouth like she was going to say something sharp, but she caught herself. "What were you doing there?"

"I was looking for Eddie."

Her face softened a little. "Did you find him?"

"Yes."

"How is he?"

"He's okay."

"Why were you looking for him?"

"I wanted to talk with him, that's all."

Ma didn't say anything. She sat down on the bed. She was going to let me be.

I looked around my room, which was small and tucked under the eaves. I kept it neat. My books were lined up on the bookshelf, my clothes were folded in the dresser, and a stuffed owl kept watch from a pedestal in the corner. Uncle Ray found it in a storage shack the college was tearing down and gave it to me. Ma always said it would bring bad luck, but I used to think that it would protect me when I went to sleep. I guess I still did.

"Ray came by yesterday," Ma said. "We were talking about you."

"Oh."

"He told me about the traps. That someone's cutting your traps."

"It could be the tide," I said.

"That wasn't what he thought."

"Well, it's hard to say."

"So what are you going to do?" Ma asked.

I got up and went to the window. On a clear day, you could see the bay and some of the islands, which looked like bumps on the horizon. Sometimes an oil tanker or a cargo ship would inch across the edge of the sea and disappear over the bend, but today it was mist, from end to end, blocking out the ocean, the islands, and the sun. No one would be lobstering today.

"I don't know."

"Is that what you were talking to Eddie about?"

"Yeah."

"What did he tell you?" she asked cautiously.

"Pull them up."

Ma nodded, letting out her breath. "That's good advice, I think." She stood up. "I know it's hard, Dain. But it's good advice. School's starting in a week. There's no sense in getting into any trouble over some traps."

She paused in the doorway. "I have to go to a meeting at church," she said. "How's your application coming?"

"I'm working on it," I said, glancing at my desk to be sure the blank application was out of sight.

"Maybe I can look it over when I get back."

"I'll see how it's coming," I said.

After Ma left, I took the application out and stared at it for about ten minutes. Finally, without having written a word, I put the cap back on the pen, found my coat, and left the house.

On the way to my truck I passed Ma's garden full of flowers. Suddenly I remembered Sonny's dad lying in one of those hospital beds Ma knew so well.

* * *

I was back at Tate's wharf, sitting in my truck. Honey was in the seat next to me with her nose out the window. I had brought her for company. The fog was out there just like yesterday, and just like the day before. It was starting to give me the creeps. It would be good to see the clear blue sky.

I got out and grabbed four empty bait buckets from the back of my truck, along with a bunch of flowers I had clipped from Ma's garden. I headed up to Tate's.

Joe Coleman and Darrell Tate stood on the porch, studying the bulletin board. Between the ads for old boats and cordwood was the notice for the meeting on the lobster fishery.

"You going to be there?" Joe asked Darrell.

"Yeah, I'll be there."

"Bureaucrats," Joe muttered.

"They think they're the experts," Darrell said, kicking some mud off his boots. "But it's the lobstermen that know what's going on."

"That's right. I've been fishing for thirty years. But do you think they're going to listen to us? What could we possibly know?"

Darrell shrugged. "Well, I've got to run a delivery into town. See you round." He gave me a nod as he headed to his truck.

I went inside with my buckets. Sonny was on the phone taking notes. It was probably someone placing an order.

I leaned against the wall watching Sonny's fingers move the pencil across the paper. They didn't seem like fingers that could throw around buckets of bait—they were long and delicate, and they moved carefully like the legs of a sandpiper picking its way across a tide pool. I looked away so she wouldn't catch me watching her hands and pretended to study a map of the bay that was tacked to the wall. But what I was really doing was listening to the sound of her pencil lead scratching on the rough paper.

Finally, the phone clanked into its cradle, and the chair scraped on the floor.

Sonny had a faraway look on her face, and she jumped slightly when she saw me. "Sorry, I didn't hear you come in." She rubbed her eyes like she hadn't slept well. "Say, what are those?" she asked, noticing the flowers.

"They're for your dad," I said, holding them up awkwardly, as if they had just appeared in my hand. "They're from my mother's garden."

"Thank you, Dain. He'll like them," Sonny said, reaching for them. "I'll put them in the walk-in cooler to keep them fresh."

She took them into the back room. "So, are those buckets for my dad, too?" she asked. It was nice to see her smile.

"No, I need some bait."

"There's no slowing you down, is there?"

"No way."

"You've got to remember to have some fun from time to time," Sonny said, taking my empty bait buckets. Her rubber boots squished on the cement floor as she went out back for the bait.

I followed her and watched as she filled the buckets.

"Sonny?"

She peered up from a barrel of salted red fish heads—the part we used for bait.

"You know someone's cutting my traps," I said.

"Yeah."

"Any idea who's doing it?"

She shook her head no. "Does someone else have their traps there?"

"No," I said, grabbing two of the buckets.

"You'd think they'd have put their traps in. Why wait?"

I shrugged. I couldn't explain it. Sonny took the other two buckets, and we went out to my truck.

"You haven't heard anything?"

"I'd tell you if I had." She put the buckets in the back of my truck.

"I think it's Roger," I said, putting the tailgate up.

"It could be," Sonny said. "He'd do it, that's for sure. And he wouldn't even need a reason."

I walked with Sonny down the wharf, where Honey was nosing around some crates.

"Have you talked to Eddie about it? Maybe he knows something," she said, taking off her baseball cap.

"I tried to last night at a party at Roger's."

"You went to a party at Roger's?" Sonny asked, surprised.

"Yeah."

"So what did Eddie say?"

"He figured I'd just pull up all my traps and get ready for school."

"So you're on your own on this?"

I remembered Eddie's angry eyes from the night before. "I guess I am."

Honey was down on a float where skiffs and dinghies were tied up. She was jumping from one to the other.

"Eddie and Roger are getting to be pretty good friends, aren't they?" Sonny asked, studying her cap like she had just found it.

"Sure they are. Eddie's living with Roger."

"I mean, they fish together a lot these days."

"Not all the time."

"No, but a lot."

"Yeah."

"So if Roger's cutting your traps, Eddie's got to know about it."

I could feel my muscles tighten.

"Maybe he's even in on it," Sonny said, still fiddling with her baseball cap.

"No way," I said, shaking my head firmly. "He hangs around with Roger, but he wouldn't be mixed up with cutting traps. Let alone *my* traps!"

"I don't know," Sonny said, putting the cap back on her head. "All I can say is I see them together. A lot."

Sonny was still watching Honey at the end of the dock. I studied the fog hanging above the trees. It had to be Roger, I thought. He could be doing it when Eddie wasn't with him. I just had to figure out what to do about it. Should I just hope it was a one-time deal and that he won't cut them again?

"Hey," Sonny yelled. "Look!"

Honey was in a dinghy, drifting away from the dock. We ran down the gangway and onto the float where the boats were tied up. Honey was standing at the back of the boat, sniffing around nervously.

I stood at the edge of the float and looked at the water where strands of seaweed were pulsing in the waves. Honey was only fifteen feet out. I could have swum for her. But a shiver went down my back at the thought of getting in the water, and my knees locked up.

Before I could even think, Sonny kicked off her boots, threw down her cap, and dove. She arched out over the water and came down with barely a splash. She disappeared underwater, and then her head popped up just behind the boat. She grabbed the bow rope and started swimming back in with the boat in tow. Honey barked. I felt like a dummy standing on the float, dry as a bone, waiting for Sonny to bring in my own dog.

Sonny pulled herself back onto the float like a seal sliding onto a rock to catch some sun. Honey hopped ashore, scampered up the gangway, and jumped into the back of my truck.

"I was going to jump," I said, embarrassed I hadn't gone in myself.

"I guess I beat you to it," Sonny said, smiling. "But I don't mind. I'll take any excuse to get in the water. Sometimes I think I could live in the ocean." She shook her head, and drops of water pattered on the dock.

We returned to the shop so Sonny could get dried off.

I was looking for a towel in my truck when Roger pulled into the lot and skidded to a stop. He and Bobby and Richard spilled out of Roger's pickup, laughing and shoving.

"Hey, look who's here," Bobby said, pointing at me.

"Guess he ain't too hung over from last night," Richard said.

"Stay here for a second," Roger said to them. He crossed the lot, taking his time, and glanced at the buckets of bait in the back of my truck. He sighed.

"I guess you're not pulling up your traps."

"No. Not yet."

"That's too bad."

"I've reset those traps I had in the Narrows," I said. "The ones you cut."

Roger snapped his eyes on me. "I didn't touch your traps," he said.

"I know you did."

Roger stepped forward. I backed up against the truck. He leaned close to me. I could feel his breath on my face. "You don't know I did anything. You think you know, but you don't."

I tried to breathe evenly and not look away.

"I warned you to get out of the Narrows when you were drifting, and I warned you again last night. I was doing you a favor, Dain. But you aren't listening too good. I *will* do something if you don't get out of there."

Roger paused, took a step back, and sighed. "You hear about what happened to Sammy Cutler this morning?" he asked like we were standing around drinking coffee at Hoppin's.

"No."

"Jeez. He got lost in the fog and ran his boat right into some ledge out by the Three Sisters. Stove a hole in it the size of your head. Water started pouring in. Sunk in minutes."

"Is he okay?"

"Sure, he's fine. His boat isn't so good, though." Roger studied his boot like he was thinking things over. "It's funny what can happen to a boat, even on a clear day. You got your dad's old boat, don't you?"

My heart leapt. "You touch my boat and I'll—"

Before I could finish the sentence Roger shoved me hard against the truck.

"You'll what?"

I'll kill you, I thought. I opened my mouth, but Roger's vacant blue eyes and the twitching muscles on his neck kept any words from escaping into the air between us. Richard and Bobby were watching and grinning from across the lot.

"Yeah, I thought so," he said.

"No one," I said, spitting out the words with conviction, "is going to push me off the water."

Roger gave me a quick look, like he was surprised I'd stand up to him, and he patted me gently on the shoulder. "That's good, Dain," he said. "That's just fine."

I started to turn away, thinking it was over, and before I could raise an arm or even flinch, Roger slugged me in the stomach. I dropped to the dirt, gasping like a dying fish. Honey barked.

Roger bent over me. "Get out of the Narrows," he hissed. "Just get out."

I heard his boots crunch on the gravel, his pickup rumble to life, and his tires spin as he tore out of the lot. Dots of light swept past my closed eyelids. I tried to pull in air, but it felt like my lungs had shut down. I felt Honey's wet nose nudge me on the cheek.

"Are you okay?" It was Sonny. She helped me get up, and I leaned against the truck.

"What did you say to him?" she asked.

"That I knew it was him cutting the traps."

"What did he say?"

"That it wasn't."

"So what are you going to do?" Sonny asked.

"I don't know."

"You could always just pull up your traps."

"Yeah, I could."

"You've got to go back to school soon, anyway."

"Yeah, you're right."

"So?"

I brushed dirt off my pants and didn't answer.

"You're not pulling them up, are you?" Sonny said.

"No."

"That's good."

"You know, Sonny, there's only one way to know for sure who's cutting my traps," I said.

"What's that?"

"Go out at night and wait. If someone's going to cut them, it'll be early in the morning."

"And what'll you do if you find out who it is?"

I shook my head. "I don't know, but at least I'll know where I stand."

I looked around the lot. It was just us, the wharf, the sea, and the fog. Nobody besides Sonny knew what was happening to me. And even though I had made up my mind, I was more than a little scared. But who wouldn't have been, going up against Roger Gribbin?

Chapter 9

When I got home, Ma was working in the garden. Uncle Ray stood beside her, stuffing tobacco into his pipe. I slipped inside before they saw me and went straight upstairs. Honey followed me up. She watched me rummage through my room. I threw my sweater in a bag with a blanket. I got a flashlight. What else did I need? Food.

Downstairs, I made two peanut butter sandwiches and took a couple of apples. I filled my thermos with coffee and put it all in my bag. As I zipped it up, Ma came in, a little red in the face, dirt on her knees. When she saw what I was doing, her face went flat, her lips tightened, and her eyes stopped blinking. Uncle Ray stood in the doorway behind her.

"Where are you going?" Ma asked.

"To Indigo Island."

"Indigo Island? Tonight?"

"Yes. I'm going to find out who's cutting my traps."

"No, you're not," she said, pointing her trowel at my heart. "You're not going out there tonight, Dain. You let those traps be."

"No, Ma. I've got to find out who's doing this."

She slammed the trowel on the table. Honey ran into the living room.

"Listen, Dain. You think you have to know, but you don't. Take it as a sign and leave it at that. The season's over. It's done. You should be bringing your traps in anyway."

She didn't understand. Ma glanced at Uncle Ray, but he kept quiet.

"I'm not going to take anything as a sign. This is my life. No one is going to push me off the water. I'm going to be a lobsterman like Dad."

Ma took a half-step back, like a boxer absorbing a quick blow.

"He was good at it," I said.

"Yes."

"So that's what I want to do."

"Dain, it's what you *think* you want to do. Wait until you get caught out there in a storm. Wait until it's so cold water freezes in your hair. Your skin peels off from frostbite. Wait until you have a bad year. Wait until you have to raise a family and leave them behind. Just ask your uncle about that. Just ask him."

She was shaking, and Uncle Ray had turned to look out the window, so I couldn't see his face.

"I don't want anything to happen to you," she said. "I couldn't stand to lose you, too."

I drew in a sharp breath. Ma always had a hundred reasons why I shouldn't lobster, but she had never said it was because of what happened to my dad.

"Don't worry, Ma," I said, trying to be comforting.

"*That* is what your father said." She turned and climbed the stairs to her bedroom.

"Ma," I called after her. I wanted to say something, anything, but nothing came out.

"Let her be," Uncle Ray said. "She needs to be by herself."

"Uncle, I've got to find out who's cutting my traps."

"I know you do."

I saw that he wasn't going to stop me. I grabbed my bag and started for the door.

"Dain," Uncle Ray said. "You be careful."

It was dusk when I pulled my skiff onto one of Indigo's little stone beaches on the side opposite the Narrows to keep it out of sight. I dragged it out of the water and up above the string of dried seaweed and driftwood, marking the high tide line.

Indigo was a long, thin island that ran alongside Pinkham's Head, a broad point of land jutting out from the mainland into the bay. The Narrows was a channel of dark water about eighty feet wide and two hundred yards long that ran between the island and the point. When the tides changed, water funneled through the channel, creating a strong current. No one else fished in the Narrows, but I'd been having good luck there. That is, until I started losing traps.

It was a scramble getting to the other side of the island: over fallen trees, down a gully, and through mounds of fern. Finally, I came to a clearing overlooking the Narrows. Just a stone's throw away were several of my buoys. There were ten in all, pulling at their lines with the rising tide.

I threw my blanket down with a sigh and grabbed a sandwich out of my bag. I was going to have to wait. There was no telling when someone would come, if they came at all. But I didn't mind. I felt like I was finally doing something. I lay back, closed my eyes, and listened. Crickets were chirruping, and a flock of herring gulls cackled as they flew out to the ledges on Pinkham's Head to settle for the night.

Above, I could see some stars through patches in the fog. The fog seemed to be lifting. It looked like the way snow gets when it blows across ice, all strung out, tugged this way and that by the wind. I pulled the blanket tighter and rolled on my side. I was remembering something from a long time ago, when Eddie still stuck by me no matter what.

It was the winter when the bay froze over smooth as glass. Everyone had gotten a little crazy from the cold, but it was all good fun. Max Leland had even driven his truck from Pottle's Neck across part of the bay to Tate's on a dare. That's how it was then.

Me and Eddie, Roger, Bobby Nuckles, Richard Grimes, Sam Higgins, Mike Keller, Louie Hoppin, and Mark Stanley all skated on the bay whenever we weren't in school. We set up boots for goals and played hockey for hours. The sound of our skates cutting the ice and the slap of the puck swirled around us and was lost in the air. It was so cold it felt like a hand was reaching into my lungs, yanking my breath away.

On one of those days, as I remember, Roger suddenly stopped playing. "Come on," he said. "Let's skate out to the islands."

"Yeah," Bobby said. "Let's go!"

I turned to Eddie. "Eddie, remember what Ma said? She didn't want us to go out past the cove."

Eddie looked at me for a second, just long enough to remember what Ma had said, and then he took off. Somebody whooped, and we were off chasing Eddie like a school of fish after its leader.

There were some clouds coming in from the west, but we didn't pay them any mind. Our eyes were on the islands, and we were feeling the perfect ice under our blades. First Eddie was in the lead, heading for Little Rock. Then Sam skated ahead. Here there were cracks running through the ice caused by changing temperatures and the currents that ran through the bay. We skated around Little Rock playing tag.

The feeling of unreality had caught all of us. It was like walking on water. This was where we fished, where we lobstered. We were on our own bay.

We went on to the next island, Whaleboat. The clouds were thickening, pushing the pale sky away. Halfway between Little Rock and Whaleboat, Bobby found a dead seal. It was frozen in the ice, with just its head and neck in the air. We stood around it, nervously edging our skate blades back and forth.

"What is it?" Richard asked.

"A seal, idiot."

"But how'd it get there?"

"Must've been an open patch, and it came up for air," Bobby suggested. "Got trapped. Right?"

The air was still. We looked across the ice, then back at the seal, its eyes, rimmed with frost, staring like beads.

"There ain't no seals around this time of year," Roger said.

"Maybe it got lost."

"Forget it," Roger said. He skated away and made a sharp turn, gaining a little speed. He took three strong strides and then pulled to a stop in front of the seal, dusting its head with white powder. It made the frozen creature even more eerie in the late afternoon light.

"Hey," I said, pointing at the sky. Dark clouds spread overhead, and it was beginning to snow. The wind picked up.

"It's getting dark," Bobby said.

"Yeah. Let's go back," Richard said.

We took off, skating against the wind. We all stayed together until we got to Little Rock. Roger said it was faster to go one way around the island, but I was sure it was quicker the other way. Everyone followed Roger, except for Eddie. He came with me.

By this time the snow was falling hard, and we could only see about twenty feet in front of us. We set off around Little Rock. The stubby island blocked some of the wind, so the skating was easier. But it was getting darker, and the snow seemed to be coming down harder, right in our eyes.

We were breathing heavily. My legs began to burn, and my secondhand skates were starting to take a toll on my ankles. I fell behind Eddie. His figure blurred in the snow. I could hear him breathing through the sound of whispering snow. My thoughts started to drift. I tried to concentrate on skating. Stride, push, stride. Stride, push, stride. The wood stove would be going at home. Dad was probably smoking his pipe, blowing smoke rings. It was a good trick, those rings chasing each other through the air. Ma would be knitting one of her sweaters, chatting with Dad about the day.

The island was on the right. We turned the point, expecting to find the other boys waiting for us, but no one was there.

"Do you think we beat them?" I asked, bent over, my hands clutching my knees.

"Maybe," Eddie said. "Let's wait a couple minutes."

We waited while I caught my breath. Eddie yelled, but his voice was smothered by the snow.

"We'd better go," he finally said. "It looks like Roger was right and they got here first. Then they must've kept going."

I looked to shore. "There aren't any lights," I said. "Nothing to aim for."

"We'll just go straight. We're bound to hit something. You can't miss the shore. It's there somewhere."

We set off into the dark, the wind blowing in our faces. My legs burned. My ankles ached. Snow collected on my eyebrows and lips. I had my head down as I concentrated on skating, listening to my blades dig into the ice.

I glanced up. Eddie had stopped again and was waiting for me.

"Come on," he said.

We stared at where the shore and the lights from the houses should have been, but there was just darkness and the swish of snow falling on the ice.

"My legs are killing me," I complained.

"I know. Mine, too."

"It can't be much farther."

"Nope."

"Okay. Let's go."

I let my mind fall silent. I just skated, putting one foot after the other. Suddenly, a hundred yards to our left, a light came on, catching the big snowflakes in their downward flight.

"It's the Mitchells' wharf!" I said.

We stood there for a moment, breathing hard. The snow was falling through the light at a slant. The air was hushed. The end of the dock and the shoreline seemed like they belonged in a world of ghosts. I was flooded by a sense of safety.

"It's beautiful," I said.

"Yeah," Eddie said. "It is."

Then we pushed off again toward the dock. I've never told anyone about the way I felt at the sight of the floodlight; I realized at that moment that the most solid things in life could disappear with no more than a whisper. Like our dad. Or Eddie.

At some point I must have drifted off. I sat bolt upright. I hadn't meant to fall asleep, but it was already dawn, and I could hear the low rumble of an engine out on the water. The boat wasn't moving fast. I threw off the blanket and dashed to the edge of the clearing. There was barely any light, and the fog was back, creeping silently across the water. It edged this way, then that way, turning solid objects into phantoms. I strained to hear the motor. It was getting closer. I looked up and down the Narrows but couldn't see a thing. I scrambled down the ledge to get closer to the water, closer to that boat. No one should be around this part of the bay so early.

I slipped on some seaweed, and a wave rolled half-way up my boot. It was high tide. I stood stock-still, trying to get a fix on the boat, but all I could see was fog. The boat was coming down the Narrows, toward me. I tried to burn the fog away with my eyes. For a second, as the fog shifted, I thought I saw the outline of the boat. Then it disappeared into the white.

I walked along the shore a bit, trying to get closer to the boat. I could hear it, the motor running slow. I bent down onto one knee and stared across the water. My muscles tightened. Suddenly, the fog shifted again, and clear as day I saw the boat, long and sleek, perfect for deep water. It was Roger's boat, the *Raptor*. There was no question, even in that light, with that fog. I let my breath out. I had my answer.

But then I saw action on the stern. It was just a blur at first, but I could tell by the way the figure moved quickly and easily that it was Eddie. In one swift move, he bent over the side, pulled up one of my buoys, and cut the rope with a knife. The buoy fell. There was a splash, and before I could think, the fog closed around my brother and he was gone.

Chapter 10

It was still early morning as I crossed the bay, returning from Indigo Island. The faint outline of Cragg Island loomed to my left through the mist. Water sloshed against the rocks. The tide was going out. An osprey perched on a jumbled nest of twigs and sticks in a pine tree at the tip of the island. I carefully noted these details, one by one, like bricks in a dam.

The outboard droned. A black-backed gull flew by, the air whistling through its feathers. Then the osprey turned its head and cried, that piercing cry that makes you think of the blade of a long, thin knife, and the picture I was trying to keep back flooded my mind: a green-and-orange buoy floating free on water black as oil and a waterlogged rope slowly drifting down toward the silent seabed where it would come to settle like death.

It was Eddie, my own brother, cutting my traps.

I felt sick to my stomach, almost hollow. I couldn't get my bearings, and it wasn't because of the fog. Everything was wrong.

I stopped the engine. I had my hands on each side of the skiff, my chin slumped onto my chest, tears running down my face. If I had just pulled up my traps like everyone had said, none of this would have happened. I would still have Eddie—the way he was, or at least the way I imagined him. Now everything I thought about Eddie was gone. I remembered Roger's raspy voice in my ear. "You don't *really* know him."

It was like a storm had washed over an island, pulling out trees by the roots. I was the island, with everything yanked right out of it.

Sloshing around inside me were other feelings, too. Anger, embarrassment. I felt like a fool. A stupid jerk. I should have seen it coming. Anyone else would have, from a mile away.

A gong buoy clanged. The waves lapped the boat. Somewhere a cormorant moaned. I drifted. Was it five minutes? Was it an hour? I really don't know. But in that time, I decided on two things: I would set my traps in the Narrows again and I would find Eddie to look him in the eye and tell him what I knew. Maybe, just maybe, he would have some explanation that I could understand, that would bring the old Eddie back.

When I got home, Ma was standing in the middle of the kitchen with a notice about the state meeting on the lobster stocks in her hand. She still wore her green nurse's scrubs, home from the hospital where she tended to the sick and their families, and maybe, for a little while, forgot about her own. She put the notice on the table.

"So, did you find out who was cutting your traps?"

The words were about to leap from my mouth, but I held them back. I couldn't tell her the truth. I could feel my heart broken inside me, and I understood that Ma had probably felt this way a hundred times, maybe more. Maybe that was why she was so hard on Eddie, to protect herself somehow from her own breaking heart.

"Naw," I said, hanging my coat on the rack by the door. "I didn't see a thing."

"Nothing happened?"

"Nothing," I said, taking a seat at the table. "It was a waste of time. It's probably just the tide taking them."

Light was coming in the window, splashing a pattern on the floor. The water in the kettle was gurgling, not quite at a boil. Everything appeared normal, the way it always did. This was my home. But inside, I was a mess. I must have looked nervous, but I think Ma was so focused on the traps that she didn't see my feet knocking against the table leg or my hand rubbing my arm.

"So what are you going to do now?"

"I'm going to keep on fishing," I said.

Her eyes hardened. "Why don't you just pull them?" she said. "School's starting in a week."

"I'm going to keep fishing. I'm doing good."

"Good?" she said, her eyes flashing. "Someone's cutting your traps, and you say you're doing good?"

"You don't know that anyone's cutting my traps," I said.

"Come on, Dain. I'm not that dumb. Neither are you."

"I can take care of myself," I said.

Her shoulders slumped. "Now you sound like Eddie," she said.

I felt bad, but not bad enough to change my mind.

"Okay, Dain," Ma said, resignation in her voice. "You keep on fishing. I won't get in your way. I'm just going to ask you to think about what you're doing. I'm telling you— you can do anything you want: go to college, get a degree, get a good job. Or you can be like Eddie."

She ended it there, and before I could answer, she went up to her bedroom.

The kettle was whistling. I made some coffee, went to my room, and sat on my bed with my head in my hands. I didn't want things to be this way: Ma upset, Eddie hurting me. I felt sick. But I had to reset my traps. I couldn't let someone push me off the water, not even Eddie. What choice did I have? I looked at my owl on its stand in the corner. It stared blankly with its glass eyes, like it didn't give a damn about me.

Standing at the end of our dock, I watched the fog shift back and forth over the water like a skittish cat. I shivered and went to the shed, relieved to be between solid walls. The fog was starting to get to me.

I turned on the light. There were tools on the pegboard, cans of paint under the workbench, nails in coffee cans. Old buoys hung from the rafters. The potbellied stove sat in the corner. Everything was in its place.

The shed smelled of salt air, sawdust, and oil. It smelled of summer. It smelled of work.

I picked through some traps at the back of the shed and pulled out the ones in the best shape. I nailed fresh lathe in the places where the traps were broken. I cut rope for the buoy lines. I found four buoys and tied them to the lines.

I tied the traps in strings and set them at the end of the dock. Then I got my bait. I rowed out to the *Rita Marie* and brought her to the dock. I loaded the traps, brought on the bait, and hopped aboard.

I went straight across the bay to the Narrows, where I found a dozen red-and-white buoys that belonged to Eddie and Roger. I didn't cut their traps; that wasn't something I could do. I simply reset mine alongside theirs in that dark, green water where the lobsters were crawling strong.

Eddie and Roger weren't going to push me out of there. No one was. If they cut my traps again, I'd set some more. This was my territory. I had every right to be there, and I'd fight for it.

I dropped the last string of traps overboard, fresh with bait, and brought the boat around, running alongside the shore, heading out of the Narrows. I felt strong and confident with my orange-and-green buoys bobbing on the sea.

I headed to Tate's wharf to get gas for the boat and more bait because I was going to be lobstering the next day and the next. I felt so good I wasn't sure when I'd stop, school or no school. Definitely not before I was ready.

On the way to Tate's, I passed Joe Coleman pulling some traps. He looked up and waved, like we all did on the water. I waved back. It was normal, like any other day, except I knew something no one else did: there was a lobster war going on, and I was in the middle of it.

As I tied up at Tate's, Sonny came out of the office and

stood on the front steps, waiting for my news. I walked down the wharf and up to the shop. I stopped at the bottom of the steps where several coils of rope were piled.

"So?" she said.

"It was them," I said. "Like you said."

"Eddie and Roger?" Sonny asked, coming down the steps.

"That's right."

"You're sure?"

"I saw it clear as day. It was Roger's boat and Eddie that cut my buoy."

"What are you going to do?"

"I reset my traps already."

"Right there in the Narrows?" Sonny picked up two coils of rope and tapped the other two with her boot.

"Right there," I said, grabbing the rope from the ground.

"They're not going to like that." We walked across the lot toward the wharf.

"*They're* not going to like it? They're the ones who cut my traps. They're the ones who started this. I've got just as much right to be there as they do. You think I should just let them cut my traps and not do anything about it?"

"I don't know, Dain. I'm just saying there's going to be trouble."

I didn't like what Sonny was saying, but she was right. There would be trouble, one way or another. But I wasn't going to back down. And neither would Roger and Eddie.

The fog seemed to be getting lighter. A breeze had picked up, blowing dried leaves across the parking lot. As they tumbled across the gravel, skittering and scraping, my confidence seemed to go with them.

"Sonny?"

"Yeah?"

"Why would he do it?"

"Who? Eddie?" Sonny asked, stacking the rope on top of some other coils on the wharf.

"Yeah. I mean, he's my own brother." I tossed my rope onto the pile.

"I know."

"Why would he cut my traps?"

"I don't know."

"Come on. He must have had a reason. He *had* to have a reason."

"Well, I heard one of the guys say Roger is having trouble making the payments on his boat. You know, he's not doing so well. I've seen the lobsters he's bringing in. Not a lot. And the Narrows . . . you've been doing real well in there. Maybe they just figure they can catch more lobsters there. Maybe they're getting desperate."

"Desperate?" I said, holding back a laugh. "Eddie's not desperate. He's the opposite of desperate. He does what he wants, when he wants. He doesn't care what anyone thinks."

"I don't think he cares about anything at all," Sonny replied. "The way he gets into fights in town. I think something's eating at him. He's not happy."

Brown seaweed rolled in the surf by the wharf. I'd never thought about Eddie as unhappy. He had it all:

friends, girlfriends; people talked about him and the things he did. It always seemed like he was gliding along as easy as can be.

We watched two gulls fight over a dead fish on the beach.

"I've got to find Eddie," I said.

"What for?"

"To settle this," I said. "If there's going to be trouble, I don't want to wait for it."

"What're you going to say?"

I laughed grimly. "I don't have a clue."

"You'll think of something."

"I better," I said, getting into my boat. "You haven't seen him, have you?"

"No. But maybe he's at the meeting on the lobster stocks."

"Are you going?" I asked. I hoped she'd be there.

"No, I'm going to visit my dad at the hospital," she said, untying the boat from the dock.

I was so caught up in my own problems, I had forgotten about Sonny's. "They're still doing tests?" I asked.

Sonny nodded.

"How's he doing?"

"He just wants to come home. He can't stand lying in bed all day."

"Are you okay?" I asked.

"I'm fine," Sonny said, holding the rope. "What about you and Eddie?"

"I'm all right."

"Just be careful with what you say to Eddie. Don't be too mad with him."

"Why not? I am mad. He cut my traps."

"Just go easy," she said, throwing the rope onto the deck. "Don't make it worse than it is."

I eased away from the dock, wondering how I could possibly make things worse than they already were. I glanced back, and Sonny was standing where I had left her, looking at the water. For a moment I felt like turning the boat around, but then I remembered Eddie and continued out of the cove.

The school parking lot was full. Cars were parked up the driveway and on the side of the road, where I found a spot. I walked across the playground, past the swing set and slide, to the school.

The gym was packed, and people were standing on their toes in the lobby, trying to hear what was being said. I pushed past them and got myself inside. The bleachers were full. People were bent forward, listening to a woman at the microphone. Four men sat beside her, two in khaki uniforms and two with ties and suits. They were probably with the state—the bureau of this, the bureau of that.

The woman's urgent voice was made tinny by the microphone. I caught some of the words. They ricocheted off the walls like shards of glass hitting on pavement. Words like "population," "decline," "overfishing," and "moratorium." I heard the individual words, but I couldn't comprehend what the woman was saying. I tried to find

Eddie in the crowd. It seemed like half the town was there: Walter Hoppin working on a sourball, Isaac Fuller staring intently at the woman's mouth, men with their arms crossed, with their hands on their knees, with mouths closed tight.

The giant light fixtures hanging from the domed ceiling crackled. There was a current running through the crowd, too. I found a spot next to Mrs. Simpson, the mail lady, and her brother, Mattie Cross, who ran a crew plowing the roads in the winter.

"There are going to be changes," Mattie whispered.

"When?" Mrs. Simpson asked.

"Who knows?" Mattie said. "Maybe this year. Maybe next. But I'll tell you, there are going to be changes."

"It's not inevitable," the lady at the microphone was saying. "There are things we can do, and we need your input to the process."

Then, a couple rows up in the bleachers, I spotted Uncle Ray and Ma. She probably came to get some points for her argument with me about college. It looked like she was taking it all in, every word the woman was saying. I worked my way through the crowd to the bleachers.

Ma moved over without saying a word, and I sat next to her.

"What do you think, Dain?" Uncle Ray whispered.

"I just got here," I said. "What are they saying?"

"They're concerned about overfishing. They say there are some signs that there's a problem, but it's too early to know for sure."

"It seems like there are plenty of lobsters to me," I said.

"Yeah," Uncle Ray said. "But someday . . . they might be right."

"Dain, are you listening to this?" Ma asked sharply, the creases around the corners of her eyes forming a web of worry.

"I'm listening," I said.

She gave me one of her hard looks. I pretended to listen for a moment.

"Seen Eddie?" I asked.

Ma shook her head.

"They're helping Roger's grandfather bring in the hay," Uncle Ray said.

Ma's face darkened. She still couldn't get used to the thought of other people knowing more about Eddie than she did. He had become a stranger to both of us.

"If Old Man Gribbin doesn't get the hay in before the rain, he could lose it all," Uncle Ray said. "It's for that horse farm—it's got to be dry or they won't take it."

"Eddie should be here for this," Ma said disapprovingly.

"Well, I'm going to go find him," I said.

"You're not going to stay?" Ma asked. "This is your so-called future they're talking about."

At that moment, I didn't care at all about my future. I was worried about the present, about Eddie and about my traps.

"I've got to talk to Eddie."

"What's so important you can't stay for this?"

"I've just got to talk to him," I said. "That's all."

I could feel her glare bore into the back of my head as I pushed my way back down the bleachers and through the crowd. The lady at the microphone droned on. The children were starting to get restless. The adults were starting to get mad. I'd read all about it in the paper.

Outside, the wind had shifted direction, and the clouds were gray like sharkskin. The air smelled of rain. I walked quickly through the parking lot, then started to jog, and then broke into a run, as if a mad dog were at my heels. I jumped into my truck and slammed the door. Once again, I had to go to the Gribbins' to find Eddie. "Roger and Eddie," I said to myself. "Eddie and Roger." My mouth went dry just saying those three words.

Chapter 11

The sign at Hoppin's General Store banged in the wind. I left my truck in the lot, dust blowing in my eyes, and walked up the woods road behind the store that went to the Gribbins' farm. I needed some time to think about what I was going to say to Eddie.

The woods were thick and dark. There was tall white pine, and spruce and birch in thickets, struggling for the light. The trees groaned and the leaves and needles rustled in the wind. The old road was barely visible beneath a carpet of pine needles and leaves. There were two ruts where the wheels of horse-drawn farm carts used to go. Now trees grew in the middle of the lane.

There was a time when farming was a way of life here and the town was mostly open field for cows to graze. When the farms died out fifty, sixty years ago, the trees crept back in, reclaiming the abandoned fields. All that was left of those old farms were the stone walls snaking through the woods that used to mark the edge of fields and the roads like the one I was walking on. Old Man Gribbin was one of the last farmers left.

As I walked, listening to the wind in the trees, a wood-pecker rapped on a tree: *bang, bang, bang, bang.* Just like the questions pounding inside my head:

Why did you cut my traps?

What's wrong with you?

What are you doing?

Who are you, really?

There was another question, too, but I didn't know if I'd have the guts to ask it. *What do you think about* me?

With that thought—that Eddie might not care about me at all—I felt a wave of anger rise up from inside me, pushing down into my arms and hands. I tightened my fists. I imagined hitting Eddie, what it would feel like, my knuckles on his chin. I saw him spin and fall to the ground. It felt good, and I walked faster, as if the wind were moving me along.

I came to a clearing where there was a small grave-yard with weeds and ferns growing between tilted and chipped headstones. A giant oak tree stood at the edge of the graveyard. The bark on the trunk was knotted and scarred, and its limbs twisted and stretched overhead.

A dozen crows, maybe more, sat in the tree's highest branches. They must have been taking shelter from the growing storm. They moved from foot to foot, watching me with unblinking eyes.

I squatted in front of a headstone and brushed aside a thorny weed. The stone was covered in lichen, rough to the touch. *Capt. Thaddeus Gribbin, born 1822, died 1859. Lost at sea. Buenos Aires, Argentina.* I read the other stones, which told similar stories of Gribbins and Perrimans and Coxes. The husbands and wives, sons and daughters. Some died young like Thaddeus Gribbin, while others lived for eighty or ninety years. They had been on whaling boats, built ships, and seen the rise and fall of the cod, the haddock, and the hake along our shores.

I looked at my feet. They were rooted to the earth. I looked at my hands. The skin on my palms was rough from fishing. There were calluses on my fingers. Pulling on rope, wrestling with lobster pots, cutting bait. This was my life. It had been my father's life. It was good, I told myself.

But here I was, with a mother who wanted me to go to college and a brother who wanted me gone. I ran my hand over the curved top of one of the stones. All I was looking for amid this unbearable fog was for my life to be clear, hard and solid like the gravestones.

A sudden gust of wind ran through the ferns, and the oak shook and groaned. I looked up, spotting the restless crows again. The tree swayed slightly, and without warning the crows took to the air. They wheeled over my head—black eyes, black beaks, black feathers—and they caught the wind, and in a breath they rose and were lifted over the trees and away to someplace beyond, where I could not see.

Behind me a branch crashed to the ground. I hurried back to the path and pushed on through the woods, thinking about what I would say and what I would do when I found Eddie. I still felt the anger in my fists. The leaves tugged and twisted in the wind at the ends of their branches. The whole world seemed to be howling.

Finally, the woods grew lighter, the trees less dense. I came to a stop in a stand of brush at the edge of the Gribbins' field, which was marked by a stone wall. Roger's grandfather was driving a rusting tractor with a trailer hitched on behind it. Eddie and Roger were throwing bales onto the back of the trailer. Bits of hay and chaff swirled in the wind.

A wall of black clouds towered in the west over faraway hills. Beneath the clouds, rain was falling, staining the sky like a purple bruise. Thunder boomed in the distance. They had only cleared half the field.

"Come on, Grandpa," I heard Roger yell. "Drive faster. Let's go."

Roger's grandfather looked to the west and gave the tractor a little more gas. If they didn't get the hay under cover, it would get soaked in the downpour and they could lose it rotting in the field.

Eddie and Roger trotted behind the trailer, grabbing bales by the twine and throwing them into the back. They had their shirts off, and even from a distance I could see the sweat run down their faces and backs. Desperation filled the air. It was a race against time.

The wind blew, the rain approached, and I stood frozen, thinking: run, go out there, help them. Roger's grandfather hadn't hurt anyone. Give him a hand. But instead I stood in the brush, at the edge of the field, and I watched them.

In a single running motion, Eddie reached down, grabbed a bale of hay by the twine, and swung it up into the air and onto the back of the trailer. By the time the bale landed in its place, Eddie was reaching for the next one. Life was so easy and fluid for him. Nothing slowed him down.

I'm sure the leaves were rustling in the wind, the branches scraping loudly, but it was all quiet to me. And cold. I knew that Eddie was being carried away to some-place beyond, and I was going to be left alone. I felt like I was at the bottom of the sea, the icy current moving slowly through the kelp, through the darkness, through the silence. The silence of the deep, deep sea. A raindrop hit me on the face, another plopped on a nearby leaf, and I turned and ran back into the trees along the old woods road. I left Eddie in the field, racing to bring in the hay, with the rain starting to fall.

Chapter 12

I stood in the lot at Tate's and watched the rain beat on the sea. A gull sat on the roof of Anson Tucker's lobster boat, its head tucked under its wing.

The rain would be drenching whatever hay was left in Old Man Gribbin's field. I started to have a hard time breathing. What had I done walking away, leaving Eddie and Roger to get in the hay? What were they going to get from Roger's granddad? Ten dollars? Fifteen? They weren't haying for the money. They were just helping an old man who had trouble making ends meet.

I wiped hair from my eyes. Water dripped down my nose. What was happening to me? They cut my traps, I reminded myself. *They* cut my traps.

But it didn't make me feel better. It sounded flat, unimportant.

I looked up and noticed Sonny's face in the office window. She was gazing across the water through the rain-splattered windowpane. She saw me and burst out the door onto the porch. She threw her arms up. "Isn't it great!" she yelled.

I gaped like an idiot.

"The rain," she said. "The rain!"

"Yeah," I said, without enthusiasm.

"It's blowing the fog out to sea. Come on. Don't tell me you're not happy."

"I'm happy."

"No, you're not."

"Sure I am."

"Prove it," she said. "Smile."

I couldn't.

"What's the matter?"

"Nothing's the matter," I said. "I need bait."

"What for?"

"I've got to fish my traps." I had to do something, anything. Lobstering was what came to mind. Hard work would make me feel better. It would drive my thoughts away.

"You can't go out in this."

"When it clears."

She gave me a funny look. "Come on inside. I'll put some coffee on."

We went into the office, and Sonny turned on the little gas stove. She cleaned two mugs and put in some instant coffee. I saw car keys on the desk and remembered that she had been to the hospital. "How's your dad?"

Her shoulders drooped. "The same. They have him on monitors and an IV." She went to the window and watched the rain. Lightning cracked out of a cloud, and a second later the pane rattled.

She turned around and tried to smile. "We've got a storm like this, and all you can think about is your traps."

I didn't answer her.

"That means you've got a problem."

"I don't have a problem."

"Sure you don't."

Of course, I did have a problem. But I was going to face it. I was going to keep fishing my traps. If Eddie cut my traps again, I'd reset them. Again and again, I'd reset them. I'd show him that he couldn't push me off the water, that he couldn't just push me out of his life without a fight.

Sonny put a mug of coffee in my hand. "So?" she said, looking at me expectantly. "Did you find Eddie?"

I blew on the coffee, hesitating.

"Eddie was out haying," I said. "I went through the woods behind Hoppin's. Eddie was out with Roger and his grandfather bringing in the hay. They'd gotten a late start on it." I found it hard to talk, the words struggling to get past a knot in my throat. I didn't want to tell Sonny what I'd done because I knew it wasn't what she would have done.

Sonny didn't say anything. She was waiting for me.

"I was watching them from the woods," I said. "And then I walked away just when the rain started. I was right there, and I could have helped them get the hay in. It's for the horse farm. It's got to be dry or the farm won't take it."

Sonny waited a moment to see if I had more to say. "Dain, it doesn't sound like you," she finally said.

There was a lull. We listened to the rain. I felt tired.

"Why did you walk away?" Sonny asked.

The question hung between us and then faded into the patter of rain on the roof.

"Why?" Sonny asked again. "Because Eddie cut your traps?"

"That's right," I said. "He doesn't care what happens to me. It's like I don't even exist. He'd do anything for Roger. But for me? All he does is cut my traps—and he knows what lobstering means to me. It's like I'm not even his brother. I'm nobody to him."

"That's not true, Dain."

"How can it not be true?"

"I'm sure Eddie didn't *want* to cut your traps. It's just those guys . . ."

"They'd do anything for each other."

"Yeah. And they're desperate. They're on the edge."

"That's no excuse, Sonny. I'd do *anything* for Eddie."

I paused, catching myself. It was a lie. A couple of weeks earlier, before anyone had started cutting traps, I would have done anything for Eddie. But since then something had happened to me.

Before Sonny could say anything or get a good look at my face, which must have been breaking up, I left the office and ran down the steps to the shore in the rain, which had settled into a steady drizzle. I looked over my shoulder. She was watching from the window.

The tide was half out, exposing slabs of rock and rafts of seaweed. I stumbled and slumped onto a piece of ledge, holding my head in my hands. I was all mixed up. "It's like I'm not even his brother," I moaned to myself.

A few minutes later I was startled by a hand on my shoulder. It was Sonny, with two diving masks in her hand.

"Come on," she said.

"Where are we going?"

"Diving."

"In this weather?"

"Sure. It's just as wet underwater."

"I don't think I want to go diving."

Sonny shrugged. "I'm going, and I think you'll like it," she said. "Darrell's going to look after things for a while."

"Sonny, I'm scared of the water. It makes me nervous." I was afraid she'd laugh, but she didn't.

"Why don't you just come along and see when we get there?"

I sighed and stood up. We walked back along the shoreline and up to the parking lot by the wharf.

"Do you have shorts?" Sonny asked.

"I've got some cutoffs in the truck."

"Why don't you put them on?"

I got in the truck and slipped on the cutoffs while Sonny went into Tate's office. When I came back, Sonny had shorts on, too, and a couple towels in a bag.

I followed her, one of the masks in my hand, across the lot and into the woods. We took a path that ran along the shoreline through stands of fir and clumps of sumac. Water beaded on the needles and dripped from the leaves. We skirted puddles that had formed in the path. I didn't ask Sonny where we were going.

It was still raining lightly when we came to Pottle's Neck. There was a stone beach littered with driftwood, seaweed, and a couple broken buoys. The tide was going out.

The water was the color of steel. Gray and lifeless.

"Under the water, just off the point, there's a pile of brick that a ship must have dumped a hundred years ago," Sonny said. "Maybe it was ballast. I don't know. But it's been there for years, and now you wouldn't believe everything that lives there. It's amazing."

"I don't know, Sonny." I didn't want to go out there. Not now, not ever, really. I had Eddie to worry about. I had me to worry about. This wasn't going to help me solve my problems.

"Come on," Sonny said, scrambling down a bank of eroding soil. On the beach, she put the mask around her neck. She waited for me to get down to the shore, and then she started wading into the water.

I pulled the mask strap over my head and followed, stepping carefully over the slippery rock. Sonny was up to her knees and then quickly to her waist.

I shook my head. What do you think you're doing? I asked myself, eyeing the seaweed pulsing beneath the waves. This is crazy. No one goes swimming in weather like this. But Sonny kept going out, not even looking back to see if I was following. She seemed so sure I would. I thought about Eddie for a moment—he'd be the first one in. And then I saw that what was happening to Eddie and me was worse than anything I'd find in the ocean, and I felt less afraid.

I stepped into the water. It was cold, biting into the tender part of the back of my knees, practically begging me to turn back.

Sonny was standing in water up to her chest, waiting. I kept going. The water was up to my thighs, my waist, my chest.

Finally, I stood next to her. I had gotten used to the water by then, and it didn't feel cold anymore.

Sonny spit in her mask and rubbed it over the glass. "It'll keep it from fogging up," she said, placing it over her face.

I spit in my mask, too, and put it over my face. It pinched around my nose and forehead.

I put my head underwater, closing my eyes halfway, afraid water would leak in and get in my eyes, but that didn't happen. The seal on the mask was tight. I looked around. My legs were white and skinny. My feet stood on rippled sand. A shrimp scuttled along the bottom. I brought my head up.

"Ready?" Sonny asked.

"I guess so."

She leaned forward and started swimming. I followed in her wake, doing the breaststroke.

We swam out beyond the point. It wasn't far, but when I glanced down, I couldn't see the bottom. Sonny paused. We were treading water, the rain falling gently, making expanding circles on the surface. Sonny looked at the point and at the beach, gauging our position.

"This is it," she said. She put her face down, rolled forward, and kicked her legs straight in the air. Her thighs, knees, and feet—pointed straight to the sky—disappeared in an instant as she dove down. I put my face under and watched her drop through the water like an arrow. She faded into the murk, but I could still see her white T-shirt. She stopped her descent, paused, and then slowly returned to the surface, bubbles trailing from her hair.

Her head emerged. "Look at this, Dain."

In her hand she held a brick. The edges were rounded from being underwater for years. It was covered with sea creatures: there were two kinds of starfish, one scarlet and small, the other with long, delicate legs attached to a body the size of a dime. There was a brown anemone pulling in its tentacles, and an orange spongy creature.

"It's a brittle star. And the spongy thing—it's a sea squirt. And there's more down there on the bricks. There's a whole colony of this stuff."

I took the brick and examined it. The starfish waved its feathery legs. I touched the sea squirt.

"Come on, Dain. You've got to see it." Sonny dove again, the brick in her hand. I watched her go back down.

I kept treading water, listening to the waves hit the shore. A gull croaked from a tree. A pine bough scraped the ledge.

I looked down again. My legs were gently kicking the water. Sonny was below me, cruising over the brick pile. It was twelve or fifteen feet deep. I was nervous, but not afraid. Sonny was there, waiting. I took a big breath, rolled forward, and dove.

Water filled my ears, and the noises from the surface were gone. I let my weight carry me down headfirst. Before I knew it, I was at the pile of brick, which spread out for yards around.

Sonny was pointing at a sea cucumber nestled in a crevice. Its billowy tentacles, shaped like the feather duster Ma used on her collection of ceramic cats, swept in the plankton. Then I saw the brittle stars, the urchins, the sponges, and fish. All this living in the nooks and crannies created by the pile of brick.

Before I knew it, I was running out of air. I pointed up and started for the surface. Sonny followed. I looked up toward the light. The rain was making rings on the surface. I could hear the drops fall *plip, plip, plip,* adding to the sea. I was in the water, surrounded by the water, held up by the water.

I broke the surface just before Sonny.

"What do you think?" she asked.

"It's amazing." I'd seen lots of things in my lobster traps besides lobsters—spider crabs, snails, and fish—but emptying a trap on the deck of your boat was different from seeing where they all lived.

"Do you want to go back to shore?" Sonny asked.

"Not yet."

We dove again, Sonny in the lead. But this time as I descended I became aware of the darkness around me. The sea was grinding rocks along the shore. Sonny was at the bottom, her face close to the brick. Beyond her, I could see a wall of kelp I hadn't noticed the first time down. It waved slowly in the current. The mask pressed against my face. I started to feel hemmed in. I glanced at the surface where it was lighter. I looked again at the kelp and the dark water beyond, and I felt a burning panic push through my arms and legs, and without thinking, I was kicking to get back to the surface. I rose as fast as I could, like I might never see the sky again. My lungs were bursting. As I kicked I thought, for a moment, that this is what it must have been like for my father when he went overboard by Trimble Island. At last I hit the surface, gasping. I started swimming for the shore, splashing madly.

"Dain?"

I paused.

"Are you okay?"

I turned. Sonny was watching me from ten yards away. I treaded water and felt the panic leave me. She swam over, the mask pushed up on her forehead.

"I got spooked," I said.

"It's okay. We should get back, anyway."

We swam toward the shore. Soon I could stand. I stepped onto the shore, dripping. Sonny gave me a towel.

The rain had stopped. As we dried off, we studied a tide pool at our feet. Bits of seaweed hung at the fringes. A hermit crab scuttled along the bottom. A starfish inched across a rock. I looked more closely and spied dozens of barnacles, their feathery arms waving in the water, snagging the tiniest forms of plankton.

"The water is so peaceful," Sonny said. "In a little pool like this or out in the bay. It always helps me think."

"That's like me on my boat," I said.

We scrambled onto the trail to go back to Tate's.

"So did you do some good thinking?" I asked.

"Yes," Sonny said, pausing to look at a cove. The tide was coming in over some clam flats. Then two great blue herons appeared from around the point, gliding over the fir trees. The birds slowed their flight, came in lower, and dropped their long legs. They disappeared into an expanse of silvery marsh grass growing along the shore.

Sonny shivered.

"Are you cold?"

"No," she said. "I was thinking about my father."

I wanted to tell Sonny that everything would be fine. He would be home soon and back on the wharf like before.

"What about your father?" she asked.

"My father?"

"Do you think about him?"

"Sometimes. Actually, that's what got me scared out there in the water. My imagination kicked in."

"I'm sorry."

"It's okay. I feel better already. I think I see what you like so much about the sea. It just might take me a little while to get used to it."

We carried on along the trail in silence. Sonny's eyes were fixed on the path.

"Sonny?"

"Yeah?"

"Your dad will be fine. You'll see."

She paused to search my face, as if I might really know the future. "I hope so," she said.

I wanted so much to make her feel better, so I took her hand and gave it a squeeze. Her face brightened, and she smiled.

"Thanks, Dain."

She started walking again, not letting go, and finally I felt like I was doing something right.

Chapter 13

The next day, it was still raining, and I didn't go lobstering. In the afternoon, the rain stopped. I found myself at our dock thinking about Sonny and wondering about Eddie.

The wind had shifted, and there was a break in the weather. The air was cool. A brilliant light cut from beneath the clouds in the west and struck the trees, the rocks, and the sea with sharp clarity. The rain had washed everything clean. It was like a new world.

I stood on our dock with a rag in my hand. My hands were greasy from cleaning the motor on my boat. I had checked the engine and changed the oil. I had scrubbed the deck, oiled the hinges, and cleaned the glass. I was hoping the work would help me sort through the jumble of thoughts in my mind, but I wasn't succeeding.

As I stared at the steely surface of the ocean, a plank on the dock creaked. I turned. It was Eddie. He walked slowly, with his even stride. He stopped a few feet from me. His eyes were bloodshot and dark. He needed to shave. His T-shirt was stained, and the bottoms of his jeans were frayed around the boots.

"She looks good," he said, running his hand along the boat. "Dad would be happy."

I wiped some grease from my hand with the rag. "I'm just cleaning her," I said.

"I can see that," Eddie said, lighting a cigarette.

I stuffed the rag in my back pocket.

"Sonny said you were looking for me," Eddie said.

I couldn't hold it in anymore. It burst out like a cork springing to the surface. "You cut my traps," I said, taking a step forward. "You cut them."

Eddie looked at me, then looked away, and he nodded his head. "I did," he said.

I waited to hear more. An explanation. His story. But Eddie just pushed a periwinkle shell with the toe of his boot. He rolled the shell until it fell through a gap between the planks on the dock.

"I wish I'd never had to do it."

"*Had* to do it? Those were *my* traps."

Eddie flicked his cigarette into the water. He rubbed his face with both hands.

"Jesus, I'm tired," he said. "I just want to sleep."

"Eddie, are you listening to me? I said you cut my traps."

"I heard you already," he said.

"Why, Eddie? Why'd you do it?"

He sighed, looking across the harbor.

"We were going through the Narrows, Roger and me. It had been a bad day fishing, a bad week. Your traps were all around. We'd heard how you'd been pulling in lots of lobsters. Roger slowed the boat down. He had an idea. Said we ought to be fishing in the Narrows, alone. You didn't need to be there; not the way we did. You were going to be pulling your traps up soon anyway, he said. Roger thought we could scare you out of there. You'd pull up your traps, and after a couple days we'd put ours down. It was easy, and no one would know it was us, he said."

"And you went along with it?"

"I thought you'd be pulling them up anyway."

"But you went along with it."

Eddie nodded.

"So just like that?"

"Yeah, it was just like that."

It wasn't a big plan or anything. They were just going through the Narrows after a bad day on the water. I bent down and rubbed my scalp, my eyes squeezed shut, trying to block out the world.

"Roger needed the money," Eddie continued, trying to explain. "If he doesn't get it, he's going to lose his boat. He couldn't get it from anyone else. Nothing was working out. I knew it wouldn't be much. What would we get taking over the Narrows? An extra eighty, ninety bucks a week? I don't know."

Eddie shook his head. He stared into the fog as if he were searching for something he'd lost out there. "Roger was letting me stay with him in the trailer. I had to do something for him. He doesn't have anyone else. Hasn't seen his father in six years. Hasn't heard from his mother in two. His grandparents are all he's got. And what can they do for him?"

"Not a lot," I said.

"No."

"So you were trying to help Roger."

"Yeah."

Waves were washing up against the pilings beneath us. "I could have loaned you money," I said. "I *am* your brother! I could've helped out."

"Like you did haying?"

Suddenly the wind and waves were hushed. Eddie knew that I left him in the rain with all those bales of hay to get in.

"Yeah, I saw you watching us at the Gribbins' field," Eddie said.

The sound rushed back to my ears. The waves pounded the shore.

"Don't worry, Dain. You probably had something on your mind. Something you needed to do. I understand."

"Did you get the hay in?" I managed to ask.

"Most of it."

"That's good," I said. I wasn't sure what else to say, so I studied the waves, watching them curl and roll onto the shore, one after the other.

Somewhere in the sound of the wind and the waves I heard Ma's raspy voice telling a story from the Bible. I finally understood what I had done in that field, why it made me feel so bad. I had betrayed my brother. It was just hay. They were only traps. But I had betrayed him by turning away when he needed me. I had excuses: I was mad he cut my traps, I was afraid that he was Roger's friend and not mine. But they were just excuses.

As we stood on the dock, not looking at each other, hands in our pockets, something was changing. Not the tide or the wind. It was between Eddie and me. He cut my traps. I walked away from the field. In those moments, in the split seconds when decisions were made, something changed forever.

Around here the waves beat the shore for months, years, decades, and slowly the changes appear: sand bars shift, rocks are rubbed smooth, shorelines erode. You can't see it happen because it's going on every moment—when you're awake, when you're asleep. Nothing can stop it.

But for Eddie and me, change happened in a breath, in the moment it takes an osprey to open its bill and cry. We changed.

"I told you at Roger's party that you don't want to be like me."

"You're the bad one?"

"That's right, Dain, I am. It's time you grew up. I'm not going to be around for you."

"I can see that, and you know something, Eddie? I don't really care anymore. I can take care of myself now. You and Roger can go on having your parties, getting in fights. No one's going to stop you."

"You don't like what I'm doing?"

I laughed. "No."

"You leave my life to me," Eddie said, his eyes suddenly flashing. "I don't need you or anyone else telling me how to run my life. Not today, not ever. Everyone's always been telling me what to do since I can remember. I might be a screwup, but I'm my own screwup, and I'm going to do it my way."

I turned away. I couldn't stand to see Eddie's eyes, wild and angry. I couldn't stand to see his lips curled around his teeth like a dog.

"If I see your traps out there," Eddie said, jabbing a finger at me, "I'll cut them again."

He turned and marched up the dock and into the woods. I pictured the crows in the graveyard catching the wind and going somewhere I'd never be able to follow.

"Wait!" I yelled.

There was no answer.

First I heard the engine, and then I saw the headlights through the pines. The truck was going slowly over the bumps of our old woods road. Grass grew between the ruts. We didn't use the road much, just to bring traps down to the dock and to take out a boat from time to time.

It was Sonny in Myron's old pickup. She rolled the window down and leaned her head out. I walked over.

"Did Eddie find you?"

"Yeah."

"How'd it go?"

"Not good."

"What did he say?"

"He said he'd keep cutting my traps."

Sonny shook her head. "What will you do?"

"I don't know."

I had my hand on her side mirror and was scraping dirt with my boot.

"Do you want to go for a drive?"

I looked up. Of course I wanted to drive around with Sonny and watch her hands move around the steering wheel as she took the bends in the road. But tonight wasn't the night for that. I had to be alone so I could let my thoughts come clear.

"Sonny, I've got to think now. Can we do it another time?"

"Anytime, Dain."

Some of her black hair was falling across her forehead, covering the corner of her eye. I wanted to brush it back into place. Maybe someday soon I'd be able to do that.

"I know you'll do the right thing," she said.

"I'm glad you think so," I said. "Because I'm not so sure."

"Dain?"

"Yeah?"

"My dad's coming home." Sonny was smiling, and it was the best thing in the world.

"Hey, that's great."

"Yeah. It looks like he'll be fine. Just like you said."

"I'm glad."

"I'll see you later," she said. "Good luck."

"Thanks."

Sonny backed the truck up and left me. Bats dipped through the air, catching insects on the fly. I went into the shed and turned on a light. All my old stuff was there: the workbench, buoys, rope, and traps. A broken dinghy leaned against the back wall. My whole life was in this old shed. But now everything was mixed up, and a lot of it was busted up.

I thought about the pile of brick Sonny had shown me off Pottle's Neck, hidden under the water. Was there more concealed in myself than I could see? Sometimes it seemed like Sonny saw things in me I didn't even know about. How could she know I'd do the right thing?

Chapter 14

I slept in the shed on a pile of rope, wrapped in a wool blanket, and woke at dawn to the rattle of the window. I rubbed my eyes and stumbled to the door to look outside. A stiff wind was blowing. Waves smashed against the shore. I closed the door against the wind and turned on a hot plate to boil some water for coffee.

I sat on a barrel by the window, watching the rain fall on the surface of the sea. The coffee grew cold in the mug as I thought about Eddie and the lobster traps, and finally I left, walking slowly through the woods to our house.

Honey met me at the door. Ma was asleep in a chair in the living room. The light was on, and her Bible had fallen from her lap to the floor. I bent down to pick it up.

"Dain, are you all right?"

Ma was awake and looking at me.

"I'm fine," I said.

"Where were you?"

"Down at the shed. I slept there."

"In the shed?"

"I was working. It was late, and I fell asleep."

She looked at me bleary eyed. She was still waking up.

"I'm sorry, Ma. I didn't mean to make you worry."

She smiled slightly. "I don't even know why I bother, between you and Eddie. You'd think I'd learn not to worry. I just can't help it, I guess."

"That's all right," I said. "I don't mind that you worry for us."

I made some coffee and brought it in. The wind blew drizzle against the picture window. It was going to be a cold, gray day.

"What are you going to do today?" Ma asked.

"I don't know," I said. "It's too windy to pull my traps."

"Pull your traps?"

"Yeah. It's time." It was the right thing to do. What was the point in fighting with Eddie over some lobster traps? In my mind I had turned this into a lobster war, but it wasn't really. If Eddie wanted to fish in the Narrows with Roger, I wasn't going to get in their way. I didn't have anything to prove anymore. Not to Eddie, not to anyone. Maybe pulling up the traps would even be a way of helping him.

Ma stared at the steaming coffee mug she held in her lap. "Dain, you're not doing it because of me?"

"No. It's time. That's all."

She looked relieved. "You're good at lobstering. I know that. But you're good at other things, too. Maybe I put too much pressure on you. I don't know."

"Ma, I'm just pulling up my traps for the season. That's all. I'll think about college. I really will."

"I know," Ma said, staring at the photo of Dad on the wall. She fell silent for a moment.

"I was hard on Eddie," she finally said. "Maybe I asked too much from him. He had to look after you when your dad died."

"He did a good job," I said.

"But who was looking after him?" Ma said. "Ray tried, but you know how Eddie is."

"Yeah," I said. "I know."

"I didn't want to be hard on you boys."

We sat for a few moments listening to the comforting sound of rain patter on the roof, until the calm was broken by the jangle of the phone. Ma answered it in the kitchen. I could hear her murmuring voice and then silence. Her voice again, different this time, and more silence. Then she stood in the doorway, the color gone from her face.

"It was Ray," she said. "Eddie's gone out with Roger. They're foundering off Indigo Island. He heard it on his radio. Roger was calling for help. Ray says the Coast Guard's on the way, but it'll take them more than an hour to get there from the station."

I jumped to my feet. We both looked through the picture window, past the bent trees and out across the darkened bay.

I took a breath, and my feet moved.

"Dain?" Ma called.

I paused at the door and turned back.

She stood, her hands clenched in a knot.

I waited for a moment. I knew what she was thinking: *For God's sake, you can't go out there, too.*

"Dain," she said. "I love you."

"I'll be back," I said.

The wind was blowing the rain and the spray straight at me. It was slanting down, pelting the cabin roof, driving against my windshield. I squinted through the glass. Feebly, the wipers swept back and forth, giving me a half-second of clear glass before it was blurry again. I couldn't see much anyway in such a downpour, so it didn't really matter. Everything was white with the rain and wind. There weren't any landmarks I could see.

I slowed the boat. I wasn't sure where I was on the water. My neck began to hurt, I was straining so hard to see through the mess. I pinched my eyes shut and took a breath.

A picture of the bay came into my head. A bird's-eye view of the islands, the ledges, the channels. The land, our house, our dock on the shore. The deep water. The areas for lobstering, the areas for fishing. I pictured my lobster run. Straight out from the mooring toward the sea to Trimble Island, around the ledges on the leeward side, a short jag to Cooper's, along the channel by Cranston, past the Three Sisters, and then a run across open water around Pinkham's Head and up the Narrows with the trees on Indigo throwing shadows across my bow.

I turned my boat and gave her gas. I cut through the water, following the map in my head. My boat pounded into the swells, *thump, thump, thump.* One after the other, they were rolling in from the wide-open sea.

With this kind of weather, no one should be out on the water. It isn't safe. You could get lost out there. Get hit by a swell the wrong way, capsize, and in twenty seconds be gone before anyone knew what had happened to you. But we were all used to those stories, and the thing was, no one—and I mean no one—thought it could ever happen to him.

I turned on the radio to see if I could pick up any chatter. Nothing.

A gong buoy clanged out toward the open sea. I was getting near Indigo. They had to be close by. I slowed, looking for them. Then, through the spray and the mist, I spotted a flash of white. It was Roger's boat.

I approached carefully. The *Raptor* was leaning danger-ously. They had run aground on a ledge about a hundred yards off Indigo Island. It was a wicked stretch of water there. At low tide the rock was exposed. Seals and cormorants planted themselves there to sleep and sun. But when the tide was high, like it was now, the ledge lurked just below the surface. They must not have seen where they were or they were too busy concentrating on fighting the waves to notice that they were drifting over by that ledge.

I brought the *Rita Marie* in as close as I could. The wind was pushing me in. I turned and steered alongside them, trying not to get too close.

Roger's boat was leaning hard. The waves were pounding into it. It didn't look good.

Eddie saw me. He waved with one arm, then with

both arms. He hit Roger. Roger looked over but quickly went back to trying to do something in the cabin.

I was about forty feet from their boat. It was difficult keeping in position with the swells and the wind trying to push me in closer to the rocks. I juggled with the gas and turned the wheel, trying to keep away from that ledge.

I yelled, "Eddie! Roger!" My voice was carried away by the wind.

Eddie was yelling, his hands cupped around his mouth. I could see his lips move, but I couldn't hear what he was saying. The wind and the rain kept beating down. I waved for them to jump. If the boat moved farther against the rock, it would be crushed, and they would be crushed with it. They had to jump and swim for it. It was too far to swim to Indigo. I was their only chance.

I waved, urging them on. Roger beat on the wheel in the cabin. The *Raptor* was his beautiful boat, and he didn't want to see her go. Who could blame him? Eddie was jawing with him, probably trying to convince him of something. Their hair was blowing. They were soaking wet.

I couldn't stay there much longer. The wind was blowing harder, and I could barely keep in position alongside them. Finally, I had to take her out and circle around, trying to get back in position. Maybe I was a little bit closer this time, thirty or thirty-five feet away.

I waved. "Roger! Eddie! Come on. Swim for it. Swim for it."

I think Eddie knew what I was saying. He grabbed Roger and shook him. He was yelling at him. Then he stood up on the side of the boat and kicked out as far as he could. When he hit the water, the splash was whipped away by the wind. He started swimming for me. Eddie was a good swimmer, but in that wind with those swells, I could see he was struggling to make any distance. His arms were flailing, splashing, wind in the air, water flying.

"Come on, Eddie!" I yelled. "Come on."

I had a life preserver right by my hand ready to throw to him when he got close enough. He was making headway, slowly getting closer, his head moving side to side, gulping for air. Pushing, pushing.

"Come on, Eddie!" I yelled again. "You can do it. A little bit further. A little bit further."

It looked like he was slowing down, his arms getting tired. How long had he been in the water? Probably only two minutes, but it seemed like an hour.

I grabbed the life preserver, judged the distance, and threw it as hard as I could. The wind beat it right down into the waves. It only went five feet and off to the side. Not nearly far enough. The preserver was already being pushed away by the wind.

"Come on, Eddie. Come on. You can do it." I was chanting like I was praying.

The wind howled. I was leaning over as far as I could, trying to get closer to him. He was only ten feet away, closer, closer. A wave crashed over his head.

"Eddie!" I yelled.

He came up for air, spitting water, gasping. Another wave smashed into the side of his head. He kept going.

"Eddie."

He reached out. Another wave crashed over his head. He went under.

I couldn't take it any longer. Without thinking, I jumped, through the air, into the cold water. Water in my ears, nostrils, underwater, bubbles running by my face. I struggled to the surface, arms flailing. Eddie went down again. I saw where he went. I was kicking, arms pumping for all I was worth. I saw his head bob up one more time, just a few feet away. I went under the water, I kicked, I reached out, and I grabbed him by the shirt and pulled him up with me. We reached the surface, gasping for air.

"Eddie, I got you. I got you."

I saw his eyes. Wide open. I grabbed him hard. He stopped struggling. My mind raced back to every swimming lesson I ever had, trying to remember anything about rescuing someone. I turned him on his back. He rolled right over. A wave washed over us. Seawater filled my mouth. I spit it out. I kicked, turned for my boat. It was only ten feet away, not far. I kicked, I kicked. The wind was pushing the boat toward us. I lunged and grabbed the side. I pushed Eddie up, and he hauled himself over with whatever strength he had left and fell onto the deck. Then he pulled me up, soaking wet, bedraggled, exhausted.

"Dain," Eddie gasped. "You shouldn't have come after us."

"Yeah, well," I said, my chest heaving, "someone had to."

I staggered to the wheel. The boat had been driven toward the rocks in just the two minutes that we were in the water together. I gave her some gas, turned the rudder, and steered away from the ledge. I got us in position again. The boat was rocking hard from the waves.

"What about Roger?" I said.

"He doesn't want to leave his boat."

"He's got to," I said.

"I know. He just doesn't want to leave it. It's all he's got, and he can't swim."

Roger couldn't swim. He had been out on the water most of his life, fishing and lobstering, and he couldn't swim. It wasn't uncommon, but Roger?

"What're we going to do?" I asked.

"I don't know."

There was only one thing to do, before the weather got worse. I turned my boat and edged her in closer.

"Get up front and look for the ledge."

Eddie didn't hesitate. He clambered up onto the bow as the boat rocked from side to side. If he slipped or we caught a wave wrong, he'd go over. He moved fast and got on his belly, his feet wedged against the rail.

Eddie waved to the left, and I moved slowly in that direction, trying to steer with the wind and the waves and the current in mind. Roger stood on the slanted deck of his boat, his hand gripping the side of the cabin, and watched us.

The wipers swept away the rain. I squinted through the glass. I could just see Eddie's back. A wave hit us, and spray flew over the bow into Eddie's face. He shook his head to get the water out of his eyes, then waved frantically. Further left. I turned the wheel hard. We were moving away from Roger. Suddenly the boat lurched, and there was a scraping noise as we hit the ledge. I turned the wheel harder, and a wave lifted us over the obstacle. A rock, wreathed in brown seaweed, passed on our right. I blew out my breath and tried to turn back toward Roger.

We picked our way across the ledge, turning slowly this way and that as Eddie guided me.

I got my boat about ten feet from Roger's. She was pointing into the wind. Eddie made his way off the bow. I waved for Roger to jump. He shook his head.

"He's not leaving that boat," Eddie said.

"Yes, he is," I said, digging through the cupboard in the cabin. I pulled out a coil of rope and a tire iron.

"What's that for?" Eddie asked.

"Uncle Ray gave it to me. In case I pulled in a shark, he said. Never needed it till now."

I tied one end of the rope to the tire iron. "Here," I said. "Throw it across to Roger."

"You do it," he said.

"You've got a better throw."

Eddie used to throw apples through the center of a tire swing we had in the backyard. He couldn't miss from twenty yards. He took the tire iron and held it up to show Roger. He gripped it by the end, cocked his arm back, and let it go. It whipped through the air, over the waves, and landed square inside Roger's boat.

Roger grabbed it. "Jump!" I yelled, my hands on the wheel, keeping her pointed into the wind and straight into the oncoming waves. The wind was starting to turn. I wouldn't be able to stay there much longer.

Roger stared at the water. A swell hit his boat and rocked it.

"Come on!" Eddie yelled.

Roger looked across at us. Eddie waved for him to jump, and finally Roger did. He took an awkward step off the side of his boat, and the wind whipped his splash away. He came up, his mouth wide open, desperately gulping air.

Eddie pulled on our end of the rope while Roger kicked. I turned the wheel and started to ease forward and away from Roger's boat.

Suddenly, a giant swell rose in front of us. "Hold on," I yelled, trying to steer into it. "We're going to get hit."

Eddie braced his feet. I gripped the wheel. Roger's eyes were wide with fear. The swell rose and smashed over us. The bow went under. We lurched to the side, toward the ledge. Eddie slipped, losing his grip on the rope. I dove across the deck and grabbed it. The rope was slack. We followed the line of rope from the boat, across the water, and into the sea. Roger wasn't there.

The air was full of noise: the wind, the waves hitting our boat, the rain beating down.

Then Roger came to the surface, spluttering, his arms flailing.

"You're almost there," Eddie yelled.

I grabbed the wheel and gave the boat a little gas, turning my side into the wind. It blew us closer to Roger.

I spun around. Eddie had the gaff. He was leaning as far as he could over the side. Roger made a grab for it. A wave hit him. He made another grab. He got it. Eddie pulled him alongside the boat, reached over, and hauled him aboard by the tops of his jeans. Roger fell on the deck, his eyes shut tight. He opened them slowly.

There was a crash and a groan, fiberglass splintering. Broken glass. "My boat," Roger moaned. "My boat."

The *Raptor* was on its side. The waves were playing with it.

I gave my boat some gas and started moving away from the wreck and the ledge, out toward the open sea where the water was deep.

Chapter 15

By the time we got to Tate's, the parking lot was full of vehicles, some with flashing lights. The rain was tapering off, and the wind wasn't blowing as hard. The storm was passing.

Ma was the first to reach us when we got to the dock. She threw her arms around Eddie, wiping hair from his face.

"Thank God," she murmured. "Are you all right?"

"Yes, Ma," Eddie said.

Uncle Ray stood behind her. Sonny was there, too, behind the sheriff and his crew.

The sheriff came forward. "Is everyone all right?" he said.

"We're fine," I said.

"Where's the boat?"

"She's gone," Roger said.

"You got insurance on her, son?" the sheriff asked.

Roger shook his head.

"Come with me, will you," the sheriff said. "We need to talk with the Coast Guard. Let them know where things stand."

Roger followed the sheriff back to his car.

Ma held me. "Are you okay, Dain?" she asked.

"I'm fine," I said.

"You shouldn't have gone out there."

"I know."

Instead of saying anything more, she held me tighter for a moment and then let me go.

"Does anyone want coffee?" Sonny asked.

Faces brightened.

"I'll make a pot," she said, turning for the office.

"I'll help," I said, leaving Uncle Ray and Ma and Eddie alone to talk. I made my way through the small crowd and started across the parking lot. Roger was slumped in the sheriff's car, his forehead pressed against the window. He seemed dazed, and his eyes barely flickered when I passed by.

I followed Sonny into the office. It was warm there and dry. It felt good to be inside, out of the wind.

Sonny took her slicker off, shaking it dry. She hung it on a peg behind the door. Then she filled the kettle from the sink and put it on the hot plate. She leaned against the desk, looked at me, and shook her head.

"You were lucky," she said.

I nodded.

"Are you and Eddie all right?"

I nodded again.

We were all right.

The water started boiling. Sonny spooned instant coffee into some mugs and poured in the hot water.

The screen door creaked open. It was Eddie.

"Just in time," Sonny said, handing him a mug. "I'll take these out to the others." She balanced several mugs on a rough board.

I held the door for her and took a mug as she went out. "Thanks, Sonny," I said.

She gave me a wink.

Eddie and I sipped our coffee for several minutes without talking. Eddie went to the window. The rain had stopped. Gulls flew past, and the tide started to turn. Brown seaweed rolled in the wash.

"You and Sonny are pretty good friends," Eddie said, sitting down by the desk.

"Yeah, I think we are."

"If I were you, I wouldn't let her get too far out of your sight."

"There's no chance of that."

I leaned against the desk. Eddie sat drinking his coffee. His hair was tangled. I noticed he had a bruise on his forehead, and his knuckles were cracked.

"Dain, I was always around for you when Dad died, wasn't I?" he asked.

"Sure you were."

He studied me for a moment, making sure I wasn't just saying something he'd want to hear.

"You know, I tried to do the right things," he said.

"I know you did."

"Well, it was never enough for Ma. There was always something else I should be doing, one more thing."

"I know."

"It was like I was never good enough, and I finally saw that I never would be."

"That's when you dropped out of high school?"

"Yeah, around there."

Eddie ran his hands through his hair. He stood up and stared out the window. "Dain, about your traps . . ."

"Forget about it, Eddie."

"Things got out of control."

"I know. It'll be okay now."

Things would be different, I thought. No one would be cutting traps or standing by when the other one needed help. Eddie would settle down, and I'd see him, not like before, but from time to time. We'd talk. We'd be friends again.

"Dain, I'm getting out of here."

"What do you mean?" I asked, alarmed.

"I'm going away. To Alaska maybe. Somewhere like that."

"Alaska?"

"Yeah. They need people to work in the canneries, on the boats."

I remembered the newspaper article he had been reading in the poultry barn at Roger's party.

"You can't go to Alaska," I said. Even after what Eddie had done, I didn't want him to leave. I thought we were going to be able to start over, fresh.

"Why not?"

"What about Ma?"

"What about her?"

I was grasping at straws. "You don't have to go," I said.

"Yeah," he said. "I do."

"Why?"

"If I don't get out of here, I'll end up like Sam Higgins."

I shuddered. Two summers ago, after a party at the gravel pit, Sam got up to eighty miles an hour on the straightaway. It was the best half-mile in town, straight as an arrow and built on a bed of crushed rock that kept it free of frost heaves in the winter. Sam lost it going through the curve at the end of the straight stretch. The skid marks are still there, running like a snake to the stand of pine at the corner.

"What are you talking about, Eddie?" I said. "You're not going to end up like that."

"I've got to get out of here," he said firmly. "It'll be better for all of us."

"We could lobster, you and me." I was desperate.

"Those days are over," Eddie said. "It's too bad, but they're gone. You don't need me around anymore."

Eddie was right of course. I could feel it. It was part of the change. Those days were gone, but I was starting to see that there would be new days and a new life before us, which could be just as good as what we had before. I closed my eyes for a moment.

"When you get there, to Alaska, I'd like to hear about it," I said. "How it is and everything."

"Don't worry, I'm not going to vanish on you," he said. "And what about you, Dain? What are you going to do?"

"Me?" I said, a hundred things leaping to mind: lobstering, Sonny, even marine biology. "First I'm pulling my traps, and then I'm finishing high school. After that it might be college, or maybe I'll take some time off. I'm not sure exactly, but I'll tell you what, Eddie, I can't wait to find out what it is. I really can't."

We left the office, pausing to stand on the porch. Sonny, Ma, and Uncle Ray were still talking by the wharf where the *Rita Marie* was tied up. The storm had passed, and the fog from the last few days was gone for good. The air felt dry and cool. Light was catching on the tips of waves in the cove and the harbor beyond.

Near Anson Tucker's lobster boat, a seal silently broke the surface of the water. Even from where we were standing you could see its eyes, its stubby snout, its nostrils flaring as it took in air. The seal rested for a moment, looked left and right, and then it dove underwater to chase schools of fish and pass through beds of kelp and swim along the channels where the currents run out to the unending sea.

"Come on," Eddie said. "Let's take your boat home."

"Sure," I said. "Let's go home."